When Will looked in the doorway, the missing part fell into place.

This was a home. A place where people were welcome. A place a person could return to feeling as if all that was important was held by these four walls.

A place where love overflowed.

Will turned away, wiping his hands, the realization rocking him to the core. He tried to fight it, tried to rationalize his way around it, but when he looked at her again, he sensed a connection, a belonging that he had never felt with any other woman before.

Books by Carolyne Aarsen

Love Inspired

Homecoming #24
Ever Faithful #33
A Bride at Last #51
The Cowboy's Bride #67
*A Family-Style Christmas #86
*A Mother at Heart #94
*A Family at Last #121
A Hero for Kelsey #133

*Stealing Home

CAROLYNE AARSEN

lives in Northern Alberta where she was born, raised and married and is currently half finished raising her family of four—if raising children is a job that's ever done.

Carolyne's writing has been honed between being a stay-at-home mother, housewife, foster mother, columnist and business partner with her husband in their cattle farm and logging business. Writing for Love Inspired has given her the chance to combine her love of romance writing with her love for the Lord.

A Hero for Kelsey

Carolyne Aarsen

Love Inspired®

Published by Steeple Hill Books™

STEEPLE HILL BOOKS

Steeple
Hill™

ISBN 0-373-87140-6

A HERO FOR KELSEY

Copyright © 2001 by Carolyne Aarsen

This edition published by arrangement with Steeple Hill Books.

® and TM are trademarks of Steeple Hill Books, used under license.
Trademarks indicated with ® are registered in the United States Patent
and Trademark Office, the Canadian Trade Marks Office and in other
countries.

Visit us at www.steeplehill.com

Printed in U.S.A.

Love and faithfulness meet together;
Righteousness and peace kiss each other.
—*Psalms* 85:10

I'd like to dedicate this book to my sisters,
Yolanda Brouwer and Laverne Van Weerden,
who've had to listen to my struggles
from thought to plot.

Chapter One

After almost three years of silence, Will Dempsey had returned to Stratton.

Kelsey Swain felt her heart fall as it missed a beat. As she watched the man standing in the entrance to the restaurant, he turned and her gaze locked with penetrating brown eyes. She clutched her coffee mug, unable to look away.

"Goodness, Kelsey, you look as if you've seen a ghost," her friend Cory said. She twisted in her chair, glancing over her shoulder, then looked back at Kelsey.

"Okay, that dark-haired fellow is one good lookin' guy," Cory said with a wry grin. "But I don't know if he merits that kind of reaction."

Kelsey tore her gaze away from Will's sharp stare back to Cory's questioning one. She blinked, trying to gather thoughts that had been scattered as easily as dust in the wind. "I'm sorry, what did you say?"

"My goodness girl, you are twitter-pated." Cory gave another quick glance back over her shoulder, then pulled a face at Kelsey. "Well, whoever he is, he's coming this way."

Kelsey's heart did another jump at the thought of facing Will once again. Too easily she remembered the last time they saw each other. At Carter's funeral. And once again she felt the all too familiar wave of sorrow followed by the sting of her husband's deception.

Though she was looking down, she felt as much as saw his tall figure walk toward them then stop by her table.

"Hello, Kelsey." His deep voice resonated, uncovering a cluster of emotions and memories.

She forced herself to look up, to meet his dark eyes and hold his steady gaze.

"Hello, Will. How are you?" The words were automatic, stilted, but what else could she say to someone she hadn't seen for three years? To her husband's former partner? To someone who, even after all this time, still brought out such conflicting feelings?

What was he doing here? Why had he come?

In spite of her questions, in spite of the welter of emotions his presence created, she couldn't help but notice the changes in him. Instead of hair that hung almost in his eyes, he now wore it shorter, smoothed back from his lean face, the dark widow's peak emphasizing his sculpted features. Instead of his usual plaid shirt and faded blue jeans, he now wore a leather jacket that flowed like butter over his broad shoulders. Khaki pants and a black shirt completed the look of business casual with more than enough money. He wore a veneer of polish and success at odds with the Will Dempsey she had known.

"I'm fine Kelsey," he replied, his voice even. "And you?"

Will may have changed on the outside, but he was the same taciturn man she knew from before. "I've been busy," she said ignoring Cory's avidly curious gaze.

"So you're back in Stratton," he said slipping one hand in the pocket of his pants.

"Yes. I live here." *Back* in Stratton? What did he mean by that?

A kick under the table from her friend startled her into remembering her manners. "I'm sorry. Will, this is my friend, Cory McKnight." She gestured to Cory. "Cory, this is Will Dempsey. He was in partnership with Carter."

Cory's gaze flicked over Kelsey's, and Kelsey could almost hear the questions churning in Cory's head. But thankfully all she did was hold out her hand to Will. "Pleased to meet you," she said smoothly. Then, to Kelsey's horror, Cory moved her chair aside in an unspoken invitation which she followed up with, "Why don't you join us?"

He glanced at Kelsey who forced a smile. It must have done the job, because Will pulled up a chair. Thankfully Cory, sensing Kelsey's discomfort, took charge of the conversation.

Kelsey kept her eyes averted, trying to find a measure of equilibrium. She hated feeling out of control, but even after three years, Will could still discompose her by doing no more than coming into the same room.

She had thought for sure Will had forgotten about her and Chris. That they had been swept out of his well-ordered life like so much debris.

It bothered her, though she knew it shouldn't. What could they possibly mean to him? He owed them nothing.

She hadn't forgotten about him, however. In the past six months, he had been more and more on her mind. Ever since she'd discovered the truth about Carter.

A couple of times she had been tempted to try to find Will. To ask him the questions that plagued her. To find out if he knew all along.

Kelsey looked at him now, as he talked to Cory, his expression composed as always. She winged up a quick prayer for strength as she tried to think of what to say to him.

"I'll get a cup of coffee for you, Will. Did you want to order anything?" Cory asked. He shook his head no.

"Coffee is fine," Will replied.

Cory got up, and as she walked behind Will, circled her thumb and finger in an exaggerated gesture of approval to her friend.

If only you knew, thought Kelsey with dismay, turning to face Will. Hoping she could manage some semblance of normal, mundane, conversation, Kelsey asked, "So what brings you to Stratton?"

Will laced his fingers together on the table, his deep-brown eyes steady. "I'm starting a road construction job just north of here. We're moving the equipment in tomorrow."

Kelsey nodded, remembering the highway expansion job that had been put up for bids a few months ago. She'd heard bits and pieces from diners in the restaurant about it getting started. It had made her think of Carter.

And Will.

"And how is the road construction business going?" She was glad she could speak with some measure of authority on what Will did for a living. She had heard Carter talk enough about Will and how he ran his father's business.

"Busy."

"You've been working all over the country again?"

He nodded, looking down at his hands. Kelsey allowed herself a moment to study him further. In spite of the emotional upheaval of seeing him again, she felt once again that disloyal tug of attraction.

Just as she had when Will would come by and visit Carter and her.

"I've got a job going in Drayton Valley as well," he said finally.

Kelsey only nodded, casting frantically about for something else to ask him, something to fill the awkward silence that hung between them.

"Mom, I'm done." Chris dropped the full salt shaker on the tray in back of her with a subdued sigh. "Now what should I do?"

Kelsey turned to her son, thankful for the diversion. "Good for you," she said with a forced smile. "You can see if Bob needs any help."

But Chris would not be distracted so easily. He looked up at Will, frowning. "Who are you?" he asked with the straightforward bluntness of a child.

Kelsey glanced at Will who was staring down at her son. She wondered if she imagined the flicker of sorrow in his eyes. Will was always so self-contained. "This is Mr. Dempsey," Kelsey said. "He used to work with your daddy."

Chris studied him a moment longer, then recognition dawned. "I know you," he said with a triumphant look. "My mommy has a picture of you with my daddy."

For the first time since Kelsey had seen Will, a smile hovered around the corner of his mouth. It was like seeing a glimpse of light on a rainy day. His face was transformed, softened and for a moment she saw a side of Will Dempsey she had seen only occasionally.

Kelsey looked away from him, unsettled by her reaction to him.

"Here's your coffee, Will." Cory set a mug down in front of Will and took a moment to ruffle Chris's hair. "Hey, sport. I suppose you'll be wanting some ice cream?" Cory glanced at Kelsey and while Kelsey would have preferred not to be alone with Will once again, her guilt over seeing her young son working won out over her own needs. She nodded her assent.

At six years of age, Chris was too young to be working after school in a restaurant, no matter how small the job. But her parents were on vacation, and she couldn't afford a baby-sitter for Chris right now. More than anything Kelsey yearned to give her son the normalcy of family life. Once Chris had two parents and security. But that ended when his father was killed driving home from work.

"Can I sit with you and Mr. Dempsey when I get my ice cream?" Chris asked, hesitating.

"Yes, if you want to."

"I do," Chris said shyly, looking up at Will with an expression akin to awe.

Kelsey supposed it had much to do with the stories Kelsey had told her young son about Carter and the work he did. Will featured occasionally in the memories so Chris knew of him.

Since Carter's death, Kelsey had done what she could to keep Carter's memory alive. As a consequence Chris had good memories of his father, and Chris loved to hear stories about him. At first Kelsey had told them gladly, though it was getting more and more difficult.

Will watched Chris leave and then turned back to Kelsey. "He looks just like Carter," he said quietly.

Kelsey held his eyes, surprised at the tinge of melancholy in his voice. It shouldn't be a total surprise. Carter and Will had been close. Once.

Some ornery streak in her, some reaction to Will's identifying Chris with his former partner made her disagree. "Actually, I think he favors my side of the family," she said quietly.

This was followed by a heavy beat of silence. Guaranteed conversation killer, Kelsey thought fiddling with her spoon.

She glanced up to see Will looking at her now, his eyes serious. "How are you doing Kelsey. Really?"

In spite of the passage of time, in spite of what she had discovered about Carter, Kelsey felt a knot of emotion tighten her throat at the sincerity in his voice.

She felt gauche as she turned the spoon in her hand, wondering how to coalesce her feelings, her anger, her sorrow into something as small as words.

"I'm doing okay. Chris and I are managing quite well," she said finally.

"Look at what Cory put on my ice cream." Chris set the china bowl with ice cream on the table with a thunk and scrambled up on the chair.

Kelsey glanced up carefully at her son's interruption. She didn't even want to reprimand him.

"Thanks, Cory," she said, sending her friend a grateful look.

Cory looked down at her, her eyebrows pulled together in a frown of concern. Kelsey shook her head imperceptibly.

"So where are you from, Will?" Cory asked,

smoothly taking hold of the conversational reins, as she sat down again.

"I'm originally from Dawson Creek. My business is based out of Spruce Grove, however, close to Edmonton."

Kelsey was surprised to hear that. When she first met Carter and Will, the business had been owned by Will's father and not really based anywhere.

"That's four hours south. You're a long ways from home," Cory said.

Will shrugged. "I only keep a maintenance yard there and my main office."

Cory glanced at Kelsey as if encouraging her to join in, but again Kelsey shook her head. She felt agitated yet, still trying to find her emotional footing.

Cory gave her a wry look, as if unable to understand how Kelsey could not want to talk to someone like Will.

Kelsey had to concede his striking good looks. As Cory and Will exchanged polite chitchat her mind went back to the first time she had seen Will Dempsey. It had been over eight years ago, in this very restaurant, a few tables down. He had been working on a job one town removed, but staying in Stratton. He was alone, and as she'd taken his order, she had tried to chat him up without much success.

He came again the next night. Again she had tried to talk to him, attracted by his dark good looks. The air of reserve that created a challenge.

That night she was rewarded by a smile that totally transformed him.

Kelsey was smitten.

Will lingered over his supper and in Kelsey's infrequent quiet moments she took the opportunity to talk to him, to try to coax another smile.

She'd succeeded. But still he said very little.

The next day he came with Carter who had joined Will after working on another job in another province.

Carter was more gregarious than Will. He bowled Kelsey over with his charm and blond good looks. He was the complete opposite of Will. And the more Carter wooed Kelsey with cards, flowers and gifts, the more reserved Will became.

Six months later, Carter and Kelsey were married. Ten months after that, Chris was born.

Carter stayed in the road construction business and Kelsey became more involved in her work in her parents' restaurant. And now and again Will would come by for a home-cooked meal. He was always quiet, always slightly aloof. In spite of his reserve, during all the upheavals in her life, she had never forgotten Will Dempsey.

A foot connecting with her shin made her look up suddenly at a frowning Cory McKnight. Kelsey pulled herself into the present, forced herself to look at Will who was sitting back in his chair watching her.

"You'll have to excuse Kelsey," Cory said, turning back to Will after lightly kicking Kelsey once more. "She's usually a lot more bubbly and cheerful, but she's got a lot on her mind."

Kelsey glared at Cory, wondering what had gotten into her friend. "Cory, stop it," she said softly, with an unmistakable note of warning in her voice.

"See," Cory said, shaking her head. "She does know how to talk. You just need to push the right buttons."

Kelsey felt tension pressing down on her, twisting her up again. Try as she might she just couldn't make casual conversation with Will. He was too tied up in her memories of Carter, and she didn't know how to separate the threads.

But to make up for her lack, she looked at him now, smiling in what she hoped was a friendly fashion.

"So where was your last job?" she asked, wondering if she was going to be forever sitting here trying to make polite conversation.

"We did an eight-month job about twenty kilometers on the Alaska Highway. On each side of the Liard River. I stayed on-site."

"In that old trailer you had?" Kelsey asked.

This brought a faint smile to his lips and once again Kelsey felt a gentle flutter of reaction. His black hair, absorbing the light, his dark eyebrows winging across his forehead, his sanguine expression softened by the gentle curl of his mouth all added up to an effortless appeal.

Kelsey pushed the thought aside, surprised at how

silly she was being and chalked it up to stress and loneliness.

"I've moved up a bit," Will replied, still smiling. "I got a travel trailer custom-made. Pull it behind my truck."

"You don't have a house?" Cory asked.

"I rent a furnished condo that I use as a base. But when I'm working I stay on-site."

"So I take it no girlfriend, either?" Cory's voice was the epitome of innocence. Kelsey easily sensed where she was going and threw Cory a warning glance.

"No. No girlfriend, either." Will laughed lightly and once again Kelsey was struck by the change in his demeanor. He seemed more relaxed around Cory. Why that bothered her, she didn't want to analyze.

"My goodness, that's too bad." Cory threw Kelsey a triumphant glance. "I think that Kelsey—"

"How long will you be on this job?" Kelsey interrupted quickly before Cory could get started on whatever it was Cory thought. It was bound to be mischief from the gleam in her friend's eye.

"This one will take about eight months. I've got another crew working close to Drayton Valley so I'll be back and forth between jobs. But I'll probably headquarter here."

The thought gave Kelsey a peculiar thrill, which she just as quickly quenched. "And then?"

Will shrugged, looking away. "I've got a few

feelers out on some other contracts in Saskatchewan.''

Other work. Gone again to a far-off place.

Will hadn't changed a bit.

''I grew up like that,'' Cory said with a crooked grin. ''It's no life. If I were you, I'd consider settling down. Stratton is as good a place as any.''

Kelsey wanted to kick her, but didn't dare. Knowing Cory, she would say something.

Will's smile grew polite. Reserved. Kelsey wondered what he was thinking.

She found out.

''Well, I've taken up enough of your time,'' he said, getting to his feet. ''It was nice meeting you,'' he inclined his head at Cory.

''I'm sure we'll be seeing you around,'' Cory said with a complacent grin. ''At least for the next little while.''

Will looked down at Chris who was absorbed in his ice cream. ''Bye, Chris,'' he said. Chris only grinned back.

Will turned to Kelsey. She couldn't stop herself from looking up at him, from meeting his level gaze.

''Take care, Will,'' she said quietly.

He paused a moment, his eyes still holding hers. ''You, too, Kelsey.'' He hesitated again. For a moment she thought he was about to say something more, then he turned and left.

Kelsey watched him go, the tension that had threaded itself around her slowly decreasing. She drew in another deep breath.

"Very, very nice, Kels," Cory said approvingly, still glancing over her shoulder at Will. She turned back to her friend. "I like the high cheekbones, the lean features. That mysterious reserve that completely transforms into devastating charm when he smiles. Why didn't you ever tell me about him before?"

"I did."

"Only in passing. My goodness, girl, he looks like a genuine hero to me."

It was their own particular joke. "The last hero through these doors was your husband Matthew. And Will is anything but a hero," Kelsey said dryly, trying to cover her own disloyal reaction to Will, wishing she could casually dismiss Cory's comments. "You weren't working here when Will used to come by. He's the original maverick. Tumbleweed. Moving on is his theme song," she said with a note of resignation. "He was Carter's partner and that was all. Once Carter was dead, I never heard from him again." Kelsey turned to Chris, signaling to Cory that the topic of Will Dempsey was exhausted. "When you're finished, Chris, Cory will take you home. I'll be by later." She glanced back at Cory, slightly exasperated with her friend. "Just make sure you don't get any of your funny ideas," Kelsey warned.

"Now, Kelsey," Cory said with a pout. "How much advice didn't you give me with my Matthew? How much pushing didn't I get from you?" She beamed. "I think it's payback time."

"Not with that man," she said definitely. "Not only is he not my type, he's not marriage material."

Cory just grinned. "He said he hasn't found a reason to settle down, that's all."

Kelsey leveled her friend a stern glance, knowing she had to nip in the bud any romantic notions Cory might have. As a single mother, Chris was her first priority. She had no other defense against men like Will. "You don't know Will Dempsey, Cory. But I do. Too well. The subject is off-limits."

Chapter Two

"**B**ut the watercourse isn't even marked properly on the prints," Will said, tucking his cell phone under his ear. He unrolled the latest set of schematics and spread them out on the drafting table that took up most of the living space in his fifth-wheel trailer.

"I don't care what some draftsman in some little cubicle seventeen floors up says," Will snapped dropping a weight down on one corner to keep the blueprints from curling, "I need a new set." He shifted the phone to his other ear, listened to a few more excuses, then ended the call. He dropped the phone on the top of the table.

"Sounds like I came at a bad time."

Will looked up from the papers in front of him to face his crew foreman, Drew Magnusson.

"Come in," Will said. "I'm just trying to iron out some unexpected glitches."

"Something bugging you?"

Will gave Drew a sharp look, wondering if his pique was that obvious. He looked back at the blueprints on the drafting table in front of him, rubbing the back of his neck. The tension that gripped his neck and shoulders he knew wasn't just from this job.

When he had submitted his bid on this project it had been with the idea that if he got it, he would have a chance to find out more about where Kelsey and her son had gone after Carter's death. He'd waited a few months after Carter's funeral and then tried to call her. But their phone had been disconnected, and he had no luck garnering any information from her parents. In fact, Kelsey's father had been very abrupt, telling him not to bother Kelsey or them anymore. He tried a couple of the larger cities nearby, but none had a phone listing for a Kelsey Swain. She had dropped out of his life.

The last thing he expected to see when he walked through the door of Hartley's Restaurant was Kelsey Hartley Swain herself.

"Hey, Dempsey. Don't get too lost in thought, you might not find your way back."

Will pulled himself back to the here and now, frowning at his foreman.

Drew leaned back in his chair giving his boss a considering look. "Did something happen to you in Stratton the other day?"

"Why do you ask?" Will picked up the blueprints and started rolling them up.

"Because you've been snappy ever since you stopped there and that's not your style."

Will shouldn't be surprised at Drew's perceptiveness. Drew had managed to see behind Will's reserve, had managed to pry loose a few of the facts of Will's life that he had not shown to anyone.

"Just tired, I guess," Will replied. He wasn't in the mood to explain his whole convoluted history with Kelsey and Carter. He didn't know if he understood it himself.

He only knew that seeing Kelsey again had been a surprise he hadn't counted on. And her sorrow had given her a haunting beauty and a distance that disturbed him.

"So you got your home sweet home all set up?"

Will caught the faint note of sarcasm in Drew's voice, sensing that his persistent friend was taking another tack. "Don't start with me, Drew. I've had enough already this morning."

"Hardly starting," Drew said with a grin. "Just continuing an ongoing discussion. One of these days you're going to have to settle down."

Kelsey's friend had said the same thing to him, Will thought shaking his head. Trouble was, lately the idea was starting to make more and more sense. For most of his life, Will had struggled not to be like his father. Instead, with each decision he made, he was getting more like him. Always moving, always busy, never in one place long enough.

"I'm sure you could find someone, somewhere," Drew continued with annoying persistence. "I mean, it's not like there's a dearth of willing women. Everywhere we go you get second looks,'' Drew said his voice taking on a puzzled tone. ''And the worst of it is you don't even try. My goodness, you hardly smile.''

Will didn't bother to answer that, hoping Drew would take the hint.

Drew waited a moment, then with a sigh, got the point. ''Okay. I'm history. But don't worry, Will, I'm not giving up on you yet.''

Drew may have been gone but his last comment lingered longer than the tinny echo of the metal door closing behind him.

With a sigh, Will sat back in his chair, looking around his trailer. It was the best money could buy. He had installed all the toys and tools—satellites for his television and phones, top-of-the-line stereo, custom-built oak cabinets, king-size bed, extralarge windows, air-conditioning. Anything that could be put into a unit this size was in it.

But no matter how you prettied it up, it was still a trailer.

Temporary.

Half his life had been spent living in trailers when he and his mother traveled with his father. The other half in a mobile home in Dawson Creek. And even when they were there, Will usually ended up staying with his grandparents to get away from the constant fighting and making up that characterized his parents' marriage.

Home hadn't been where the heart was, he

thought. He picked up the prints and pulled out another set. But even as he tried to get involved in his work, he couldn't stop himself from thinking back to what Drew had said.

Couldn't stop from thinking about Kelsey who, since he saw her again, had hovered on the periphery of his mind. Whether he liked it or not, they were linked through their past.

And whether he liked it or not, he wanted to see her again.

"One of these days I'm going to get a plaque engraved with your name on it, Anton, and rivet it to this table." Kelsey stood with her arms crossed, taking a moment to laugh with Anton and Ed, two very regular customers.

"It would be the only right thing to do. Ed and I keep this place going." Anton tipped his stained baseball cap farther back on his balding head and grinned up at Kelsey.

Kelsey's eyes flicked to the half-empty coffee cups in front of each of them. "Not just drinking coffee, you don't."

"Not fair," Anton sniffed with a wounded air. "Yesterday I ordered pie. And left a tip."

"Wow, Anton, what happened? A rich uncle die and leave you all his money?" She laughed.

"Yeah. And I'm going to buy this restaurant and then you won't have to worry about the bank."

Kelsey felt the familiar heaviness return. Anton might have been joking, but her worries about the bank were increasing the more she dug into the convoluted bookkeeping system her father had created. The restaurant wasn't technically for sale, but unless a miracle occurred, it would be the next step. "If you buy it," she said aiming for her usual bantering tone, "I'll run it for you."

"And do a great job." Anton nodded with assurance. "I wouldn't worry, Kelsey, you'll pull the restaurant out of this slump. It's such a great place."

"Don't forget the great customers," Kelsey added.

"The best," Anton said, resettling his bulk in the chair. "Besides, you can't leave. Who is going to give me my morning hug?"

Kelsey rolled her eyes. "As if you ever got one, Anton."

"I live in hope." Anton laid a massive hand on the front of his plaid shirt, fluttering his stubby eyelashes up at her.

Kelsey smiled, and laid her hand on his shoulder. "Hope away, my dear man." She turned, still grinning and as she looked up, her step faltered.

A couple of tables away, sat Will Dempsey, his dark head bent over a menu. Today he wore a white T-shirt and blue jeans. A complete contrast to what he had looked like when he had first come to the restaurant a few days ago. Today he looked more like the man she remembered.

She recovered both her step and the smile as she wondered what he was doing here.

"Good afternoon, Will, have you ordered already?'' Kelsey asked, immensely pleased with the easy tone in her voice.

Will looked up at her, his dark eyes somber. ''Yes, I did. I thought I would come in for some supper.''

''Considering this is a restaurant, I would say you've come to the right place,'' she returned with a polite smile.

''I heard it's a good place to eat,'' he said, resting his bare elbows on the table, his hands clasped in front of him as his direct gaze pinned hers. She saw a flicker of hesitation, of uncertainty, then he blinked and she knew she had imagined it. Will's life and his actions had always been straightforward with no apology or explanation.

She nodded as she held his dark eyes, disturbed by the emotional turmoil his calm presence created in her, and at the same time wondering what it would take to get a smile out of him. ''I can personally recommend this place,'' she said, looking away.

At that moment Chris bounded up beside her. ''Hi, Mom. I'm done in the kitchen.'' He paused, looking sidelong. His eyes got bigger. ''Hi, Mr. Dempsey,'' Chris said in a hushed tone. ''You come to have supper here?''

As Will looked over at Chris, Kelsey could see his features soften. ''Yes I have, Chris.''

''Don't you eat at your own house?''

Will smiled at that. Kelsey's heart fluttered in response. She bit her lip, once again angry at how silly she was being. She who should know better.

"Sometimes I do," Will replied, "But I don't like my own cooking."

Chris nodded, as if understanding that perfectly. "I can make eggs," he announced. "But that's all. I fry them. Do you like eggs?"

Will nodded, his expression bemused.

"I could make some for you sometime," Chris said, raising his eyebrows in invitation. "In your house."

Kelsey put a warning hand on her son's shoulder, sensing Chris's next conversational gambit. Chris was shameless in wangling invitations to other people's places.

"What did you want, Chris?" Kelsey asked, abruptly steering him away from that topic.

"Billy wants me to come to his house Saturday. Can I, Mom?"

Kelsey fingered her son's hair, as she bit her lip. Billy Dansworth was three years older than Chris and not the most suitable company for her young child.

"I have to work, sweetie," she temporized, wishing this discussion didn't have to take place in front of Will. She could predict what was coming.

"But it's Saturday. I don't wanna be here all day," he complained, dropping his head.

Kelsey put her hand on her son's shoulder, applying gentle pressure. She was fully aware of Will's eyes on them and wanted to continue this elsewhere.

"Chris, honey, come with me to my office and we'll talk about it."

"No, Mom," he blurted, twisting his shoulder away from her hand. "I don't wanna talk. I wanna go to Billy's."

Kelsey closed her eyes, praying for patience, praying for respite from her constant companion as a single mother—guilt.

"Honey, please."

Chris turned to Will. "Did you have to work in a restaurant when you was little?"

Will looked momentarily taken aback. "No, I didn't."

Chris turned to his mother, as if Will's comment clinched it. "See Mom. He never did. And he used to work with my dad. And he was my dad's friend. And he never had to work in a restaurant."

Kelsey frowned at the convoluted logic, again embarrassed that this had to happen in front of Will.

"I had to do other work, though," Will said quietly.

This stopped Chris. He angled a curious glance at Will. "What kind of work?"

Will leaned forward, his elbows on his knees, hands clasped loosely between them. "I had to help roll up hoses and clean off equipment. When I was six, I had to help put ribbons on stakes. All kinds of things. Even on Saturday."

Kelsey couldn't help but listen, trying to imagine Will as a young boy. Wondering what his life was like. Carter had alluded to it on occasion, but he didn't know much, either. Will had always been a puzzle to her, he gave away so little.

Chris looked mollified as he listened to Will. Then he looked back at his mother, and heaved a sigh. "But I still don't want to come here."

"I know, sweetheart. But that's the way it is."

With a quick nod of acknowledgment, Chris turned around and trudged off to the kitchen.

Kelsey turned to Will, who still sat in his chair, but was now looking up at her. "I'm sorry you had to see that," she said, "but thanks for telling him that you had to work, too. It put things into perspective for him." And gave her something she never had from her parents or many other adults beside Cory and Matthew.

Support.

Will rested his elbows on the table and gestured to the chair across from him. "Do you want to sit down?"

She stiffened. She couldn't help it. The idea of sitting with Will Dempsey was tempting. How long had it been since she had spent any time with another man?

But now? With someone who had the same job and lifestyle as Carter had? Most unwise. "I'm sorry," she said, lifting one hand in an apologetic gesture. "I've got too much work to do. Maybe another time?"

"Maybe," Will agreed, sitting back in his chair.

Kelsey gave him a quick smile, then walked past him, her heart pounding in reaction. She stepped into the office and leaned back against the door as she willed her heart to settle down.

Too many emotions, she thought, closing her eyes as she slowly regained control. Too much on her mind.

She took a deep breath as she walked to her desk and slowly sat in the chair.

She turned her chair around, facing the family picture she had taken just before Carter's death. Carter held Chris on his lap and she stood behind him, her hands resting on his shoulder. As if she owned him.

What a joke.

Around the picture were some cards, a few dried flowers that Kelsey kept meaning to take down. When Cory had worked at the diner, she'd teased Kelsey, calling it the shrine. Whenever Carter was away he would send her flowers and cards and phone her. She used to think it was love.

Now she was sure it was guilt.

She got up and with a few quick tugs, pulled the dried flowers away and took the cards down.

She even contemplated taking the picture down, but knew Chris would ask, her parents would wonder. She had pushed herself in this corner, she thought. Everyone thought she was still crazy about Carter. And once she had been.

She threw the remnants of her dreams into a garbage can and once again fingered the keys at her waist. Easily she caught the one that belonged to a dented metal box she had found buried in a forgotten corner of Carter's workshop. It had taken her a few years, but finally, she had gone to the basement and cleaned the entire corner out. That was when she found the box.

"Don't do this," she whispered, even as she pressed the catch to release the ring of keys. Biting her lips, she found the key. She got up, walked into the storage room behind her office and got the box. Returning to her desk, she set it down and opened it.

When Kelsey first found the box, she'd gone through the old papers with a measure of nostalgia. Then she found the letters in an unfamiliar handwriting. She had opened one at random.

It was from a woman named Connie. And it was addressed to Carter.

She picked it up now, anger surging through her once again as she reread the words of betrayal.

"...And when are you coming again? I miss you so much, lover. Or are you trying to make sure Kelsey doesn't find out about us? Someday you'll have to tell her. Someday she'll need to know the truth...."

Kelsey dropped the letter in her lap, knowing that no matter how she twisted the words, they were what she thought. A letter from a woman who was having a clandestine relationship with a man.

It had been only six months since she had discovered Carter's perfidy. Yet, if she were honest, her suspicions had been aroused long before. She just never wanted to face them. His long absences. His distracted air when he did come home.

Yes, he had showered her with flowers and cards. Yes, he had called her almost every day when he was working. Pain and sorrow and anger twisted through her. Surely that counted for something?

She thought of the man who was now sitting in the restaurant only a few steps away. Will. Did he know all about Carter? Did he know what had been happening?

Oh, Lord, please help me through this, she prayed, pressing her fingers to her eyes. *I have Chris to think of and he needs me now. Carter is gone. It shouldn't matter anymore.*

But it did. She felt like a fool. She had worked so hard to keep Carter's memory alive for Chris, for her parents—and he didn't deserve it. Why even knowing what she did about Carter, she had made plans to take Chris to his father's grave tomorrow on the anniversary of Carter's death.

She knew she could never tell Chris the truth. And it was her own fault. She had defended Carter, had built him up. Deep down, she must have known how shaky the foundation was that she was building on, but she kept on. Overcompensating for Carter's long absences, his job. The lack of time he had spent with her, with Chris. It was all for Chris. So he would have some positive memory of a father he barely knew.

At times it wore her out. Stifling a light sigh, Kelsey set the picture down, brought the box back to the storage room, promising herself that soon she would throw it away. Before her parents found it.

She returned to her desk, trying to concentrate on her work. But she couldn't. Will's return to Stratton had distracted her, had brought up old memories that she had been struggling to deal with these past months.

She pulled open another drawer and pulled out her Bible and turned to Romans 5. "Not only so, but we also rejoice in our sufferings, because we know that suffering produces perseverance; perseverance character; and character hope. And hope does not disappoint us."

Hope. Kelsey leaned back and sighed a little. Hope was what sustained her through the dark days after Carter died. Hope and a faith that God would never leave her, never forsake her.

She had to fight the shame that engulfed her each time she thought of all the tears she'd shed for a faithless husband. Thankfully, God was faithful.

But oh, how it hurt yet. To discover this after Carter was gone. To be denied some kind of revenge, a chance to even up the score.

She stopped that thought, biting her lip. She had gone through anger over and over again, and it was literally eating away at her. It had to end.

Kelsey read on a bit more, craving the peace that God's words could give her, then closed the Bible and put it away. Time to get back to work. To face a whole different set of worries.

She let herself dwell briefly on the upcoming

meeting with their account manager at the bank. It was supposed to happen once Bill and Donita came back from their vacation.

Her stomach twisted as she thought of the financial juggling she was proposing. It was a long shot, to save the restaurant, but it could work.

It had to work.

She had Chris depending on her.

She took a quick breath thinking of her son. Chris. He was her first priority. The gift God had given her to help her through her grief. The reason and force that kept her going to school after Carter's death, kept her working here.

It was all for Chris. She knew now that only God was able to give her the unconditional love she received from her son.

She knew that no man could.

Chapter Three

"**W**hy do you seek the living among the dead?"
The quote drifted from nowhere into Will's mind as
he parked his truck on the graveled lot just beside
the graveyard entrance. He hadn't been here since
the funeral. Today, Will wasn't sure if it was guilt
or obligation that brought him.

Will pushed open the metal gate, as if to push the
memory aside. The gravel crunched beneath his feet
in the stillness of the afternoon. He stood a moment,
trying to recall where the grave was relative to this
gate.

He walked a little ways up and then turned, guessing. He read a few names, none of them known to
him. Then, there it was. A simple brown stone with
Carter's name, date of birth and death. Beneath it a
Bible verse.

"The Lord brings death and makes alive." I Samuel 2:6.

The passage seemed out of place amongst stones that held quotes of comfort from Psalms. He knew from the times his grandmother read to him that Samuel was a book about King Saul and David. Mighty men.

Stories of betrayal and mistrust.

Will knelt down in front of the stone, touching it as if to reinforce the reality of Carter's death. He traced the words of Samuel and realized, that whether it was done intentionally or not, the book the quote was taken from was apt.

The drone of another vehicle's engine broke the quiet of the graveyard. Will got up, glancing over his shoulder as the small car parked beside his truck.

Kelsey and Chris. He didn't want to intrude on their grief, but it would be rude to leave now.

"You've got the flowers, Chris?" he heard Kelsey ask as she got out of the car.

"Whose truck is that, Mom?" he heard Chris ask.

"It's Mr. Dempsey's." He wondered if he imagined the cool note in her voice.

He stayed where he was as they walked through the already open gate. Chris saw him and came running, clutching a large bouquet of daisies and carnations.

"Look what I have, Mr. Dempsey," Chris said as he skidded to a halt in front of Will. He held up the flowers and grinned. "These are for my dad's grave. It's right behind you. Did you see it already?"

"I did," Will said, smiling lightly at Chris, marveling at the little boy's complete lack of self-consciousness. He truly was just like his father, at ease in most circumstances.

Kelsey approached them more slowly, her hands shoved in the pockets of her khaki pants, her peach-colored sweater accenting the bronze highlights in her hair.

She wore it loose today, framing her face. Her cheeks were lightly flushed, her green eyes dulled by some indefinable emotion. "Hello, Will," she said quietly, her glance holding his a moment then slipping away.

"Hello, Kelsey," he returned, wishing he could say something else, wishing for a moment, that he had Carter's ease with words.

Instead he stepped aside, making way for her.

"Shall I just lay the flowers down, Mommy?" Chris asked.

Kelsey nodded, but made no move to step closer to the grave, or to help her son. He squatted down, setting the flowers out in a fan in front of the headstone. Then he jumped up, looking at Will. "Are you here to see my daddy, too?" he asked.

Will only nodded.

"We miss my daddy a lot," Chris said with a heavy sigh. "My mommy is sad today."

Will was surprised at the quick stab of jealousy he felt at Chris's words.

"Mr. Dempsey doesn't need to know that, Chris," Kelsey said softly.

Will couldn't see her face past the copper-colored curtain of hair. He wondered if she was crying now.

"I'm sorry, Kelsey," he said. "It must be hard at times."

She shrugged, still looking away.

"Was my daddy a good man?" Chris asked Will.

"Chris," Kelsey admonished lightly. "Mr. Dempsey might not want to talk about Daddy."

Kelsey was right, but Will couldn't brush aside the pleading look on Chris's face.

"Your daddy was a hard worker," Will said truthfully.

Chris nodded. "My mommy has lots of pictures of my daddy," he said, his expression somber. "She has a picture of him on a Caterpillar." He tilted his head, as if considering Will. "Do you know how to drive a Caterpillar like my dad did?"

Sorrow mixed with melancholy flicked through Will at the note in Chris's voice. Pride for an unknown father combined with the yearning for more information about him.

"Yes, I do," Will said, glancing once again at Kelsey. He couldn't help himself. She stood like a sentinel, avoiding his gaze. Lost in her sorrow he presumed.

He wondered what it would take to get her to turn around and look at him. To look at him the way she used to look at Carter.

"Do you still have the Cat my dad drove?" Chris asked.

Will pulled his attention back to the little boy and he squatted down, getting to his level. "I do." Then on impulse he said, "Would you like to see it some-time?"

Chris's eyes got huge, and he stared at Will as if he had just given him Christmas and a birthday all wrapped in one. "Can I? Really?"

Will nodded, but then glanced at Kelsey who was finally looking at him, her expression unreadable. "If it's okay with your mother?" Will asked, directing the question to her.

"I don't know," Kelsey said slowly, turning to her son. "I can't bring you there, Chris. I don't have time."

"I can come and pick him up," Will said suddenly. "Maybe this Saturday."

She glanced at him again. "I—I'm not sure...."

"But, Mom," Chris pleaded. "I want so bad to see what my dad did."

"I know, honey."

Kelsey's gaze flicked to Carter's headstone then back to her son as she twirled a piece of hair around her forefinger. Will remembered the little nervous habit from long ago. She did it whenever she was worried.

The familiarity of the gesture gently unearthed feelings he thought he had dealt with. Usually, when he'd seen Kelsey, it had been with Carter right there. And each time he had experienced a mixture of emotions. Jealousy for the obvious devotion that she showed Carter, mixed with a faint disdain that she couldn't see Carter for what he was.

Carter was gone now, but from what he had seen,

he was still very much a part of Kelsey and Chris's life.

"I'll take good care of him, Kelsey," he said softly. "Just like I did when he was a baby."

Kelsey blinked, then glanced back up at him, a careful smile on her soft lips. "I remember that."

"He was just this tiny little thing," Will said drawing out the memory. "I was always afraid to hold him. A man's usual fear of babies, I guess."

"Well, you didn't drop him," she said with a full-fledged smile. She looked back at her son. "I know he would love to come with you. He's been talking about Carter more lately. I wish…" She let the sentence trail off as she looked away again.

Will felt it again. That faint press of jealousy for a man who had been dead for three years. A man who didn't deserve the unswerving loyalty of this beautiful woman.

"Can I go look at the other stones, Mom?" Chris asked.

Kelsey nodded. As he skipped away, Will thought Kelsey might leave, but instead she stayed where she was.

"You don't have to take him, Will." Kelsey tucked a strand of hair behind her ear as she glanced back up at him. "Chris can be a little pushy at times."

"I don't mind at all."

She smiled at that and to Will it was like a physical touch. "I know he'd far sooner be tramping through the mud of a construction site than wandering around the restaurant doing some silly chore I've dreamed up for him.''

She clasped her arms across her stomach as her eyes flicked back to her son.

"He's a good kid, Kelsey," Will said. "You've done well with him."

"Thanks for saying so. I think I'm always struggling with the feeling that I'm not doing enough for him."

"It must be difficult handling it all alone."

"It can be, yet I'm so thankful for him. God has blessed me richly. But I guess because I'm doing this alone I never feel like I'm doing enough."

"You've never thought of remarrying?" As soon as Will asked the question, he wished he could retract it. He wondered what she must think.

Kelsey shrugged lightly, avoiding the question.

Will didn't push the issue. It shouldn't matter, but for some indefinable reason, it did.

"I should be going." Kelsey flicked a quick glance Will's way. "So you'll be coming tomorrow?"

"Yes. Where do you live?" Will asked.

"Same place I always have." Kelsey frowned at him. "Well, except the years I was studying in the city."

Will felt puzzled as her words sunk in. "You lived in the city?" he asked, surprised at this revelation.

"Yes." Kelsey looked up at him, puzzled at his question. "After Carter died, I went for two years to college there and took some business management courses.''

That's why her home phone was cut off. That's why he couldn't contact her.

He wondered why Bill Hartley wouldn't give out that particular piece of information when Will had called him.

Will pushed those thoughts aside. ''I'll pick Chris up before you go to the restaurant.''

''You might want to wait until I'm at the restaurant.'' Kelsey paused, a faint smile slipping over her features. ''I remember Carter saying how much you hated getting up early on Saturdays.''

''How early do you leave?''

''I leave for the restaurant at six.''

Will tried not to look horrified, tried not to wince. ''That is an insane time to get up on a Saturday,'' he said slowly.

''I can take him with me. You can pick him up later.''

Will shook his head. ''If that poor kid has to be up that early on a Saturday morning, it certainly isn't so he can get taken to a restaurant. I'll just have to consider it a rescue mission.''

Kelsey's smile grew. ''This will make him happy, Will. I really appreciate you doing this.''

Will couldn't help the kick of response at her broadening smile. She looked more like the Kelsey he remembered. ''I do it gladly, Kelsey,'' he said.

''Hey, Mom. I found someone else with

Grandpa's last name,'' Chris called out from across the graveyard. He waved to her to come over.

"I better go," she said, effectively dismissing him. "See you Saturday."

He nodded and watched as she walked over to where her son squatted. She had a quiet reserve about her that she hadn't before. Kelsey had always been so outgoing and friendly. Losing Carter had obviously been a blow from which she hadn't yet fully recovered.

"That's a trackhoe. It's like a backhoe, but bigger. And see? The backhoe has wheels that move it. The trackhoe has a track. Just like a Caterpillar," Will explained to Chris who sat in the truck with him, wide-eyed in amazement. Around them earthmovers growled and Caterpillars snarled in what seemed to be senseless movement.

The radio crackled as the operators of various machinery rattled off bewildering chatter.

Chris's head swiveled around, as if unable to take in the absolute power of all the machines surrounding them.

"Did my dad drive those?"

"Yes, he did," Will said leaning back in his seat. He was amazed how much he was enjoying this morning. When he had first offered, it was partly out of pity for a young boy having to spend his Saturdays keeping busy. Will himself had spent many a Saturday and Sunday as well working with his father. But if he were to be honest with himself, it was also for Kelsey. To help her out just a little. He was actually surprised she allowed Chris to accompany him.

"Can I ride on the earthmover?" Chris asked, breathless with excitement.

"No. I'm sorry, Chris. It's too dangerous."

"Please?" He turned to Will, his whole expression one of pleading. "Please?"

He could just imagine what Workers' Comp would have to say about a young child sitting in the cab of a Cat. "Even if I wanted to, I couldn't. It's illegal," he said.

"Just for a little minute?" Chris changed tactics and opened his eyes wide, the picture of innocence. "I won't touch anything, I won't talk too much."

Will shook his head in amazement. The boy had the same charming persistence that was the hallmark of his father.

Poor Kelsey.

"No, Chris. And I don't want to hear any more about it."

Chris sat back, his head down as he picked at a tiny hole in his pants. But thankfully he said nothing more.

Will had never dealt with young kids. The rules weren't so clearly defined. There was no blueprint to follow. It would probably be easier if he treated him like an employee. Arm's length and keep the emotions out of the situation.

Just the way he handled everything else. But it wasn't as easy. Chris was an engaging young child.

And he was Kelsey and Carter's son.

"Let's go see what some of the other guys are doing," he said, putting the truck in gear. He glanced at his watch. Kelsey said she would be coming around four to pick up Chris. It was already three-thirty. He didn't want to be too far away when she came.

This morning when he had come to pick up Chris, she had been friendly and slightly more outgoing than she had been since he had first come. He found himself looking forward to seeing her again.

"The camp is just across the creek. As soon as you cross it, turn left." The flag girl pushed her hard hat back on her head, her smile a flash of white against her bronzed skin. "Mr. Dempsey's trailer is the white one with the deep-green swirls on the side. If he's not there, you might have to drive a little farther down the road."

"Thanks," Kelsey smiled at her, and pressed the button to roll up the window. Except it didn't work. Again.

After speaking into her two-way radio, the flag girl waved her on.

As Kelsey drove, she alternately looked out for a creek and kept trying to close the window. One more thing to add to the broken-down list she thought with a flash of annoyance. A list that already had a fallen window box, a garden hose minus an end and a sink that still drained slow. There were times she was tempted to sell the house and move into an apartment. But she loved the idea that Chris had a yard to play in. Sure the payments were steep, but once things got turned around at the restaurant, she was sure she could pay down some of the mortgage.

Kelsey crossed the creek but found no sign of a road that led either left or right.

She drove a little farther, momentarily regretting the impulse that led her here. This morning Will had offered to bring Chris back, but years of doing things on her own had made her say she would pick Chris up.

Besides, like a typical mother, she'd had niggling doubts all day about how Chris was behaving. He could be demanding and stubborn, and Will had no experience with young children.

Finally she saw a glint of metal through the trees and she turned down the graveled approach into the campsite. Trailers and fifth-wheel units ringed a central campfire. A yellow, rectangular aluminum trailer stood to one side. The office, Kelsey remembered from visiting Carter on-site.

When they were first married, she had offered to come and live with him on-site, but he preferred that she stay in Stratton, saying it really wasn't much of a life. Knowing what she did now about Carter, his preferences made more sense.

She parked her car and spotted, what she presumed, was Will's trailer. It was a long unit with a slide out, tucked away against some trees, isolated from the rest.

Just like Will, she thought with a wry smile. A

loner, who didn't seem to need people the way most people did. For a moment she wondered about girl-friends. Surely someone as arresting as Will would have had his share of female admirers.

The thought didn't sit well.

She looked around a moment, reluctant to go up to either Will's trailer or the office trailer. When no one showed up after a couple of minutes, she started her car again, looking around the site once more. With the completion of the job, this minitown would be no more. Will's gleaming fifth-wheel trailer would be parked on another site in another part of the country.

Temporary. No responsibility other than to the job.

She shivered, then brushed the premonition away as she drove out of the compound. She had enough to think and worry about without letting someone like Will occupy her time. Sure he was good-looking and yes, if she were honest, appealing. She appreciated his taking Chris off her hands today, but she didn't need to complicate her life by falling for the physical charms of a man as reserved as Will. A man as temporary as Will. A man who did the same thing Carter did and who was probably subjected to the same temptations.

Farther down the road the roar of equipment grew louder. She rounded a bend in the road and slowed down. She saw a group of trucks parked on an approach. One of them was a deep-green truck with the symbol of Will's company emblazoned on the door.

A group of men clustered around a parked Caterpillar, having an animated discussion.

As Kelsey pulled up behind the truck, she spied her son. Or at least she assumed it was Chris. From her angle it looked like a hard hat perched on a pair of skinny legs.

Chris stood beside Will who had crouched down, gesturing at something under the Caterpillar. As Kelsey watched, Chris edged closer to Will, his hand snaking over to catch Will's gloved one.

Kelsey could see Will smile as he adjusted Chris's hard hat. Then he was looking back at the underside of the Cat, all business again.

But he maintained his hold on Chris's hand, and Chris kept looking up at him with undisguised admiration.

A sudden memory intruded.

Will gingerly holding the tiny swaddled bundle that was Chris. He was looking down at the baby with a peculiar expression. Hunger, Kelsey had thought at the time and when Will had looked up at her, his face was once more reserved.

But she had seen that flash of weakness, and it had endeared him to her.

Now, once again, Chris was standing with Will and this time it was Chris who looked up at Will with that same hungry expression.

For a moment Kelsey wondered what she had done, allowing a man like Will into her son's life.

But it had happened and she just prayed that when Will left again, she would be able to explain to Chris that this was what Will did. Come and go.

He was a man's man, she thought, feeling a sudden chill of recognition. She had seen enough of them pass through the restaurant. Long-haul truckers, oilfield workers. Never in one place long enough to put down roots. Impermanent and transient. There was no such thing as a hero. Carter had tarnished that particular dream. Will had the potential to destroy it completely.

Chapter Four

"Hey Kelsey, you found us," Will said, tugging off his gloves as he noticed her. His eyes, darker than ever beneath the shadow of his hard hat, caught hers. Slowly he straightened, pushing his hat farther back on his head. His frown faded, his expression lightened. But it was his smile, spreading across his face that made her heart stop.

Warm, welcoming. It was as if he had been waiting for her, waiting to bestow the gift of his smile on her. Only her.

Kelsey caught herself up short, dismissing the foolish reaction. She was just here to pick up her son, not make eyes at a construction worker like some foolish girl.

Chris whirled around. "Hi, Mom." He ran up to her, all the news of the day spilling out in a torrent of words.

"Will let me sit in a trackhoe. We're fixing the Cat now," he enthused as he caught her hands, pulling her toward the disabled machine. "And we watched earthmovers and other Cats and I saw some stakes and Will gave me some ribbon and, and..." He paused as if unable to articulate all the wonders of the day in something as small as words.

Will stayed where he was, as if waiting for her. In spite of her resolve, his smile drew her on like a baited hook.

"Hello, Will," Kelsey said, tossing her hair back from her face as she stopped in front of him, determined to face him down, to treat him like she always had. "Sounds like Chris has had quite a day."

Will glanced down at Chris, giving his hard hat a little thump. "He's been helping me."

Kelsey grinned back, canting her head sideways to look at the Cat behind him. "Caterpillars are his specialty."

"Our next step was to get him to crawl underneath it and have a look at the oil pan."

"Of course," Kelsey said, playing along with the joke. "And I presume you'll want him to show up on Monday morning for trackhoe duty."

Will laughed aloud at that. The warm sound gladdened her heart.

Against her will, her gaze slipped sideways, into his. Mistake, she thought as he held her eyes, his own intent. She couldn't look away, knew she had to.

"Will?" One of the men held up a cellular phone. "It's the mechanic. He's on his way."

Will gave Kelsey a quick, intense look, as if apologizing for the intrusion, pulled off his gloves and took the phone.

Kelsey felt a moment's relief, knowing that she was stuck with a bad combination of loneliness in the presence of an attractive man.

"Can I come back here again, Mom? After school on Monday?" Chris asked.

"No, honey," Kelsey said, smiling at the sight of the hard hat slipping to the back of her son's head. "It's too far to drive you, and Will is too busy to pick you up."

Chris dropped his head, carefully pulling his hand out of Kelsey's. He poked at a rock with the toe of his running shoe. "I'd really like to," he said softly.

Kelsey stifled a sigh as once again guilt washed over her. Chris had his moments, but overall he wasn't a complainer.

"What would you like to do?" Will asked, shutting the cell phone and handing it back to one of the men with him.

Chris looked back at Will, his eyes full of hope. "I wanna come here, but Mom says I can't."

Will frowned at Kelsey. "I'm sorry, did I do something I shouldn't?"

"Not at all and I really appreciate what you have all done," Kelsey hastened to assure him. "He was talking about coming here after school and that's not going to work."

"Could he come Saturday again?"

Kelsey hesitated, feeling torn. She had gotten so much done today with him gone. But she didn't think it was wise to involve herself any more than necessary in Will Dempsey.

"Can I, Mom? Please?"

Kelsey heard the plea in her young son's voice and knew what the alternative was to coming here. She would just have to keep Will at a distance. Something that shouldn't be too difficult these days.

"I suppose you could," she said carefully. "If you are as good as Will said you were today."

Chris's mood swung instantly from sadness to wonder. "I will be," he crowed. "I will."

"But—" Will held up a warning hand "—only if you promise not to complain during the week about having to help your mother."

Kelsey caught herself in time from protesting Will's admonition to her son. After all, she had entrusted Will with Chris for an entire day and was going to do so again. She could hardly complain when he put a few conditions on the deal.

"So, help your mom and next Saturday, if it's okay, you can come here again. Deal?" Will held out his hand, begrimed with oil and Chris slipped his own into it. They shook solemnly.

"Okay, now that's settled," Kelsey said, feeling a motherly need to intervene. "I think we should be moving along, Chris."

Chris shook his head. "Not yet, Mom. Will promised me I could—'' He stopped when Will laid a warning hand on his shoulder.

"You'll be here next week," he promised.

Chris nodded. "I won't see you until Saturday?" he asked.

"Probably not."

Kelsey's senses took a dip at Will's cryptic reply. It shouldn't matter to her, she reprimanded herself.

"We won't see you on Sunday?" Chris asked with the innocence of a young child.

"I don't think so."

His answer nailed down one more reason Kelsey should keep her senses around this man.

"Why don't you come to church?" Chris asked with the guilelessness of a child. In his circle, most everyone went to church on Sunday.

"Chris, I don't think Will wants to talk about that right now," Kelsey chided him.

"No. That's okay," Will said, his glance catching Kelsey's eyes and then cutting back to Chris. "Do you have a church in Stratton?"

"Yes. Me and Mom go every Sunday."

"That's good," he said quietly. "Church is a good place to be on Sunday."

"Why don't you come?" Chris pressed.

Kelsey thought she should stop him, but on the other hand, she was curious to hear what he would say.

"I might," he said, nodding his head slightly. "I just might."

Silence followed his comment. Chris was apparently satisfied and Kelsey wasn't ready to pursue this any further.

"Thanks again for taking him," she said, squinting up at Will. "It made my day a lot easier, and I know he had a marvelous time."

"Glad to help." He pulled his gloves out of his back pocket and slapped them against his pant leg, looking as if he had something more to say.

Kelsey waited, a sense of expectation in the air.

But then he pulled his gloves on, avoiding her eyes. "I'll see you next week," Will said to Chris. "And maybe you'd better give that hard hat back to me."

Chris pulled it off and handed it to Will, his expression full of awe.

Kelsey gently nudged Chris, suppressing another prick of disappointment at Will's comment. "What do you say to Mr. Dempsey?" she asked.

"Thanks. Thanks for everything." Chris positively beamed up at him.

"You're welcome." Will turned the hat over in his hands, gave Kelsey a quick glance. "It was good to see you again, Kelsey," he said, then turned and strode away.

Kelsey watched him as he joined the men. Watched as once again he hunkered down. She wondered why she let her eyes linger on him, why she stopped to watch someone who treated her so offhand. Was she letting herself be put into a very vulnerable position yet again? Hadn't she learned her lesson?

"C'mon, squirt. Let's go home." She caught Chris's hand, almost pulling him along.

Chris wasn't looking where he was going, his head turned around, as if unable to keep his eyes off Will as he stumbled along beside his mother. Kelsey looked down at her son.

I know how you feel, she thought wryly, wishing she dared look back so blatantly. But Chris's interest was childish hero worship.

Allowing herself any kind of interest in a single man as attractive and elusive as Will, would prove to be dangerous. She had more than enough to deal with right now.

"Can we go to the cabin, Mommy?"

"Pardon me?" Kelsey pulled her thoughts back to her son.

"I want to show you the cabin. The cabin Will showed me today."

"Oh, honey, I don't know."

"Please, Mom. It's not far."

Kelsey looked down at her young son and again felt the guilt that was her constant companion. She and Chris spent so little time together just having fun. "Okay. As long as it doesn't take too long."

Soon they were bumping down the rough grade of the approach, down into the ditch.

She turned off the engine and as they stepped out of the car, Kelsey took a slow breath, letting the quiet pervade the busyness of her soul. A light wind soughed through the trees, beckoning her.

"We have to go down here," Chris said, tugging

on Kelsey's hand as he plunged down a trail into the silent welcoming woods.

Kelsey smiled as she followed her son, his infectious enthusiasm spilling over onto her. The trail forked, and Chris confidently took the right fork. Overhead the trees softened the afternoon sun, creating cool shade. Their feet barely made a sound on the soft dirt.

Other trails broke off this one, but Chris forged on ahead.

"Are you sure you know where you're going?" Kelsey asked, feeling a moment's hesitation. They had been walking for a while now.

"It's just pretty soon here. I member that tree that falled-down there." He marched confidently on, and Kelsey followed. She had kept track of how they had come. If he couldn't find the cabin she would have a pretty good idea of how to find their way back.

Finally they came to a small clearing in the trees. In the center of the clearing sat a small plank-sided building. A large overhang protected the porch, which ran along the front.

"Isn't it neat?" Chris said running toward it. "Will said we can't go in, but we can look inside." Chris jumped onto the porch, tugged on the door and with a creak of wood against wood, it opened.

"Be careful, Chris," Kelsey warned with the automatic words of motherhood.

Kelsey followed him and peeked over his shoulder. The cabin smelled of wood and smoke and looked inviting.

"I think we should sleep here one night," Chris said. He looked back at Kelsey. "Can we?"

"Maybe," Kelsey temporized. She glanced at her watch. "But now, we really have to go."

Chris grabbed her hand and grinned up at her. "Isn't Will a good finder?" he said, obviously proud of his new friend. "He showed it to me."

"Yes, Will is a good finder," Kelsey agreed, her son's pride in Will creating a curious mixture of pleasure and pain.

"So, what'll you have?" The waitress parked herself by Will's table as she pulled an order pad out of her apron without even looking at him. She had a hard-edged attractiveness negated by her brassy blond hair and lipstick worn to a thin red outline on her lips.

"The steak sandwich," he said, handing her the menu.

She wrote it down, the only acknowledgment Will had that she had heard him. Then as she took his menu, she glanced at him, then gave him a second look.

He finally got a smile out of her.

"That's a good choice," she said, tucking the menu under her arm. "I often order that one, too."

"Then you should be good at it," he said, disliking the sudden change in her. He wondered how much Kelsey knew about her staff. If he was running this place he'd have this girl fired in a heartbeat. Each time he had come here she was either lolling around one of the booths, chatting up her friends, or standing outside, smoking a cigarette.

The petulant look returned as she realized he was poking fun at her.

As she left, Will wondered how long it was going to take for his supper to come. Might have been quicker to just pick up the parts he needed and go to his trailer to eat.

But the thought was unappealing.

So here he was, sitting in the same place he had the last time he had come. From this vantage point, he could see most of the restaurant. It was often full. This time of the day, waitresses were scurrying back and forth.

"Will, you came again." Chris bounded up beside him, his smile almost splitting his face. "I thought we wouldn't see you until Saturday."

"I had to come into town for parts and thought I would stop and have a bite to eat."

"Just one bite?" Chris asked, puzzled.

"Probably a bunch of bites," Will said, unable to stop the grin at Chris's quirky humor. "Where's your mom?"

Chris sighed. "She's sitting in the office. Hitting the calculator."

"Pardon me?" He had visions of Kelsey banging on a machine. "You mean she's adding up numbers on it," he corrected.

Chris shook his head, his expression solemn. "Nope. She's hitting it. It's making mistakes."

"How do you know?"

"Because she says 'you dumb machine, that can't be right.' That's how I know. Then she hits it. I want to get her a calculator that works."

Will heard more behind the little boy's assertion than a dysfunctional calculator. Stratton wasn't big and though he hadn't spent much time here, he'd been on the hind end of a few conversations while conducting business in town. One or two of them had been about the financial woes of the Hartley Restaurant.

"Maybe you can come and fix it for my mom," Chris said, grabbing Will's hand.

Will was about to resist. After all, the restaurant's problems weren't his, neither were Kelsey's. He didn't need to get tangled up in either.

But Chris looked so concerned, that he decided to play along. Besides, in spite of keeping his distance, part of him wanted to see Kelsey in her own milieu.

Chris pulled him along and without knocking, burst into the restaurant's office.

As Will entered, he saw Kelsey sitting behind the desk her fingers flying over the buttons of the miscreant calculator. Her hair hung loose around her shoulders, framing her face in an aureole of copper. Her flushed cheeks and bright eyes attested to her difficulties.

Paper spilled out of the calculator at a furious rate, joining the two-foot-high pile in front of her desk.

She hit a key, and as the machine rattled out the total, she pulled a pencil from behind her ear and glared at the calculator at the same time. "That has to be wrong," she said through clenched teeth.

"Mom," Chris said in a subdued voice. "Will is here."

Kelsey's gaze flew up. She dropped the pencil. She stared at Will as if unable to comprehend his presence.

Then she straightened her shoulders and sat up. Will found he far preferred this side of Kelsey. Spunky, alive. Much like the woman she was when he would come and visit.

"What can I do for you?" she asked, tucking her hair behind her ear in a movement reminiscent of the waitress he saw only a few moments ago.

But where that girl's action looked slovenly, on Kelsey it made her look defenseless. Made her look endearing.

"I'm sorry," he said quietly. "I can see this is a bad time. Chris thought I could fix your calculator for you."

Kelsey sat back in her chair, pulling her hair back from her face with both hands as she frowned lightly. "Fix my calculator?"

"Mommy, Will can fix Cats and stuff."

Kelsey blinked, then turned to her son who was now standing beside her. "I'm sorry, Chris. I don't understand."

"I told Will your calculator isn't working."

Then Kelsey smiled. "Unfortunately, it's working

all too well, son.'' She glanced back at Will as Chris climbed up on her lap. "So what brings you to town?"

He rocked back on his heels, suddenly averse to leaving her alone. "Thought I would get some supper here. I like the food."

She leaned back, slipping her arms around her son, almost absently. Will could see these were familiar motions for both mother and son as Chris began to toy with her hair. Their ease with each other created a soft ache that he tried unsuccessfully to dispel.

Had his mother ever held him like that? Or had she been so caught up in trying to please her father that she forgot she had a son?

"So can I ask what the problem is with the calculator?" he asked, dismissing the useless questions.

Kelsey glanced up at him and bit her lip. "Like I said, the calculator works fine." She hesitated, then shrugged. "Just having a little trouble balancing the books. I just took them over from my father, and I'm just trying to learn his system. One of the many things I've had to learn."

"And the others are...?" Will prompted.

Kelsey pulled a face. "Firing people. I need to cut staff. My father hired anyone who walked through the door with a long face and a sad story. All I have to figure out is who to get rid of." Kelsey tilted her head to the side as if taking his measure. "You're a businessman, Will," she said softly,

"How do you get rid of someone that you know isn't doing their job?"

Will felt pleased that she had asked his advice. Each time she had been with him it was like she edged away from him, not able to trust him. This was the first time she showed some sign of their old relationship.

Hooking a chair from behind him, he sat down as he considered her question. "Have you given him or her a warning?"

"Yes." Kelsey shook her head, her fingers threading through her son's hair. "A couple of times."

"So. Then you very calmly approach this person and tell them that after the next pay period, they don't need to bother coming back. Simple as that."

Kelsey laid her chin on Chris's head, looking past Will as if considering his words.

"Simple as that," she repeated softly.

Will could tell she wasn't going to be up to the job. "If you don't mind to take some advice, I would recommend that you get rid of the waitress with the black roots and the attitude."

"Lorelei," she sighed. "I know. I've told Dad any number of times to get rid of her, but he's not firm enough."

"Your parents still on vacation?"

"Yes they are...." Kelsey's sentence drifted off as she stroked Chris's head with her chin. Chris seemed more than content to just sit there, listening to conversation Will was sure he couldn't follow.

He sensed Kelsey wanted to say something more and he wanted to hear it. He glanced at the paper in the calculator, thought of her frustration, the conversations he had heard and put them all together. "Is the restaurant having trouble?"

Kelsey dipped her shoulder, prevaricating. "Let's just say that my father has never been the most ambitious of businessmen."

"Can you pull out of it?"

Kelsey sighed lightly. "I had hoped so."

He easily caught her use of the past tense. "Not anymore?"

"I'm meeting with the banker. I'll know then how bad the damage is."

"You sound tired."

She didn't look at him, and he knew he was right. "I am. This place keeps me busy all hours." She sighed lightly again.

"Why do you stay?"

"I've lived here all my life," she said. "My parents put everything they owned into this place. I don't know anything else but restaurant work. This is where I always wanted to be." She glanced down at Chris. "This is where I was married, this is where Chris was born. When Carter and I bought the house here, I thought I had everything God could possibly have given me all in this place."

Will felt a moment of bittersweet pain at the mention of her husband's name. *Carter, what had you thrown away?*

"You've never wanted to live anywhere else?"

"Carter always talked about moving to Stony Plain, but I didn't want to. I lived in the city when Chris was small and hated it. I could hardly wait to get back here. I was hoping to do more extensive studies," Kelsey continued, "but I already had too much debt, I couldn't afford to borrow any more against the house. So I came home."

"Why did you have debt? I thought it could have been paid off?"

"With what?" Kelsey laughed lightly.

"The insurance money."

"What insurance money?" Now Kelsey returned his puzzled look.

"The insurance money you would have received when Carter died."

Kelsey blinked, then straightened. "I didn't get any insurance money, Will."

Chapter Five

Will plunged his hands through his hair, staring at Kelsey as if to verify what she said.

"You didn't get any money?" he repeated.

"No. Nothing."

Will felt a cold shiver trickle down his spine as the implications of what she said settled in. "I can't believe he did it," he said softly.

"Did what? What are you talking about?"

A picture on the wall behind Kelsey caught his eyes. The Carter Swain family. Kelsey and her beloved husband. And what would she have to say about him now?

"Will, what insurance money are you talking about?" she prompted softly.

Will took a slow breath and sat back in the chair, hoping, praying he could explain without shattering her illusions. She would neither thank him, nor appreciate him for it. It shouldn't matter, but the more time he spent with her, the more it did.

"Will. Please tell me," she urged.

Will leaned forward, his elbows on his knees, his hands dangling between them as he tried to find the right words.

"When we started the business," he said quietly, "we both took out insurance policies, to cover each other. We increased the coverage after you married Carter." He looked up at her then, holding her troubled gaze. "The amount would easily have been enough to pay off the house and give you something extra besides."

Kelsey was shaking her head slowly, a frown creasing her forehead. "So why didn't I get it?"

Will bit his lip, considering what to tell her. "It was a whole life policy, an investment as well as a life insurance policy," he said. "By that time we'd had it long enough that he could get some of the money back again. Just before he died he had been talking about cashing it in."

Kelsey lowered her eyes, her hands still fiddling with her son's hair. "I see." She was silent a moment, then dropped a quick kiss on Chris's head. "Well, I don't have it and I guess I won't find out."

He didn't want her to let Carter off so easy. Something made him go on.

"You might find out if you go looking, Kelsey." He tried to keep the challenge out of his voice. Carter didn't deserve this kind of devotion and for some reason he didn't want to explore right now, he wanted her to at least ask a few questions.

Kelsey didn't look up at him, and Will sensed that the subject of Carter was closed.

"I should go." He stood. "I'm sure my dinner is on the table by now."

Kelsey just nodded absently in acknowledgment, holding Chris close to her as if for protection.

Will glanced at her, then back at the pictures of Carter.

For a moment he envied Carter for Kelsey's unswerving devotion, blind as it may be.

"Take care, Kelsey," he said quietly. Then he turned and left.

You should have told her everything, he thought, as he walked back to the table. And how should he have told her, with Carter's picture on the wall, with her holding Carter's son on her lap? What difference would it have made? Carter was dead.

He wasn't sure why he wanted her to see Carter for who he was. Wasn't sure why it should matter.

He just knew that he was jealous of a dead man.

Will stopped at his table and looked at the place setting that had been put out for him while he was with Kelsey.

He wasn't hungry anymore.

He picked up his discarded jacket from the chair beside him. Tilting sideways, he pulled his wallet out of his pocket and dropped some bills on the table.

Then he left.

* * *

Kelsey stood by the window, hugging herself. Behind her Chris fooled with her "broken calculator."

She had dismissed Will's questions about the insurance money but she couldn't forget about it. Nor could she erase the fresh hurt at yet another sign of her husband's disloyalty not only to her, but their son.

How could he? she thought, clutching the sleeve of her sweater. What had he done with it? Given it to Connie?

She thought again of Carter's long absences, the harried phone calls from places that didn't always jive with where he was working. The times he was at home, but withdrawn, almost sullen. She would tease him out of those moods, but it seemed that there were moments he resented being home.

She had passed off her doubts as disloyal and had quenched them. But she had no doubts anymore.

Kelsey fought the anger that engulfed her, the shame, the frustration. She thought she had dealt with all of that. It was as if each time she felt she had come to some sort of equilibrium, something else came her way to bring up the past.

What do you want me to do, Lord? Hate him again and again? I'm so tired of feeling this anger over him. It's over. It's over.

But even as she prayed, she couldn't forget what Will had told her.

She turned back to the window surprised to see Will stride toward his truck, his denim jacket slung

over his shoulder, anchored with his thumb. He had
that self-confident air that stopped just short of a
swagger.

She thought he was going to have supper. He
must have changed his mind.

Just before he got into his truck, he paused, glancing back at the restaurant.

"Mommy, why are you watching Will?"

Kelsey pulled back from the window, a sudden
flush warming her cheeks. She looked down at her
son who had suddenly materialized beside her.

"I'm just…uh…waving goodbye."

Chris just nodded as if this were very normal.
"Can we have some supper now? I want a hamburger today."

"Okay," Kelsey stroked his head, thankful he
had believed her little evasion. She cringed thinking
about other stories she had been telling him. Stories
about a father who didn't deserve to be remembered.
"You go find a place to sit, and I'll be right there."

Chris ran out the door. Kelsey could not resist
another look as Will drove away, his profile somber
as ever.

She gave her head a shake. Will was even more
of an enigma that Carter. She was being utterly foolish weaving any kind of daydreams around him.

Kelsey spent the next few days continuing the job
of working her way backward through her father's
bookkeeping system.

The restaurant shouldn't be losing money, she

knew that from handling the cash flow of the past six months. Figuring in just the day-to-day income and expenses, they should be coming ahead.

She knew part of the ongoing problem was an entire year of defaulted loan payments, approximately three to four years ago. The interest on interest, coupled with a higher than usual payroll was crippling them.

The only trouble was, Kelsey had never been able to figure out how her father had missed on the loan payments. He never gave her many details. All she could get out of him was a downturn in the local economy had caused the restaurant severe financial difficulty. The only other option open to her was to go through the confusing bookkeeping system. Once again Kelsey wished her father had used an accountant like most businesses did.

By Saturday morning, Kelsey didn't want to see another canceled check, another bank statement. She had become increasingly short-tempered with her parents, away on this ludicrous vacation, frustrated with her son who constantly asked when Will was coming and with herself for not doing what the minister had urged them to do the past Sunday.

To let God's grace permeate through her life. To let the amazing gift of salvation color all her actions and thoughts. To forgive. To carry on.

Which was easier said than allowed, thought Kelsey, pushing her hair back from her face.

She looked up at the door, thinking of Lorelei and knowing she couldn't put off her next job any longer. She had dreaded it all week but knew that she had to lay off some of the staff.

And fire one or two others.

This moment was her best chance, she realized. Chris was busy in the back "helping" Bob with some baking and would be occupied for the next few minutes at any rate. Will wasn't coming to pick him up for a while. The restaurant was quiet. She would be undisturbed.

Kelsey took a deep breath, sent up a prayer for courage as she stepped over a stack of bank statements from three years previous. She smoothed her hand over her hair, over the gray suit that made her feel more like a boss and walked out into the restaurant.

How fortunate, she thought, spying her first "problem."

"Lorelei," Kelsey called out. "I'd like to talk to you in my office, please?"

Lorelei looked up from the crossword puzzle she was doing at an empty table and frowned. "Sure." She closed the book and followed Kelsey.

Kelsey's heart fluttered with nervousness. Her hands were like ice as she prayed once more for strength to see this through. She had never done this before.

Lorelei shut the door behind her and immediately dropped into the chair by Kelsey's desk.

"So, whaddya want to talk to me about?"

Kelsey remained standing, preferring to deal with this situation from a position of authority. "Remember I spoke to you a couple of weeks ago about your attitude?'' she said, keeping her voice quiet, controlled.

Lorelei shrugged. Her action was an easy dismissal of that conversation and another reminder to Kelsey of why this girl had to go.

''I'm afraid that it has been brought to my attention that things haven't changed.'' Kelsey folded her arms across her chest hoping she looked in control. ''I'm sorry, but you are going to have to leave.''

Lorelei raised glittering blue eyes to hers and in spite of her resolve Kelsey was taken aback at the malice in her expression. ''You firing me?'' Lorelei asked, her voice rising.

Kelsey squeezed her arms tight against her sides, her heart thudding heavily in her chest. ''Yes,'' she managed to reply, forcing a calm she didn't feel into her voice. ''Yes, I am.''

''Why?''

''As I said before, your attitude is the main reason.''

Lorelei slouched back in her chair.

''I've been here a long time. Wasn't a problem before.''

''My father didn't want to see it as a problem. I have different plans for this place.''

Lorelei laughed, but it wasn't a pleasant sound. ''Yeah. Big plans. Carter told me that.''

Kelsey felt an icy shiver drift down her spine. ''What did you say?''

''You heard me.'' Lorelei carefully inspected her

nails. "You weren't the only one Carter talked to, you know." She gave Kelsey a sly look, rife with double meanings. "I talked to him lots." She looked back at her nails. "Lots," she repeated.

While part of her wanted to yell that what Lorelei implied wasn't true, another part of her acknowledged Lorelei's brassy good looks. Carter might have considered her attractive. Might have spent time with her.

She felt her stomach roil, her heart begin to pound with anger, humiliation. *Help me through this, Lord,* she prayed. *Please let me hold it together until she leaves.*

"Whatever conversation you may have had with Carter has no meaning," Kelsey said, forcing herself to stay focused on the job at hand. "I'm still firing you."

Lorelei jumped up and for a split second Kelsey thought she was going to attack her. Instead, she stood facing Kelsey, glaring at her, her eyes like ice chips. She took a quick breath, then another.

"Did you really believe all those cards that he sent you? Did you really think that when he was gone he was always alone?" Lorelei snarled. "You're a fool, Kelsey. He was never faithful to you. Never." Then she yanked off her apron, threw it on the floor at Kelsey's feet. Whirling around, she stormed out of the office, slamming the door behind her.

Kelsey wilted against the desk, biting her lip against the sudden wave of emotions.

It was just words, she reminded herself. Lorelei had just told her words and how did Kelsey know they were true?

Of course they're true, you fool, Kelsey castigated herself. Connie, Lorelei. She bit her lip against a new onslaught of humiliating tears. Must she face this again and again? Was God trying to grind her nose in her husband's unfaithfulness?

Forgive me, Lord, she prayed. Forgive me. I hate him so much right now.

Kelsey took a deep breath as heaviness settled in her chest. *Please, Lord. Don't let Chris find this out. Don't let him know about his father.*

Suddenly everything seemed too much. Keeping the restaurant going, trying to get her father more involved, trying to be a good mother to Chris who even now was playing in a restaurant kitchen while he waited for a man who wasn't his father to take him someplace.

She thought of Will and stiffened. Carter's partner. His friend. He had known something about the insurance money. Had he known the truth about their marriage?

It was too mortifying to contemplate.

The soft knock on the door sounded like thunder in the concentrated stillness of the office.

She spun around, grabbing an invoice pad from her desk, pretending to be studying it's empty lines. She didn't want anyone to see her like this. All she needed was a couple of minutes to pull herself together.

"Who is it?" she asked, her voice heavy with suppressed emotions.

The door creaked open, and Kelsey glanced over her shoulder.

Will stood framed in the doorway, his one hand slung in the back pocket of his blue jeans.

Her heart plummeted. Of all people, she had to face him. She couldn't handle this right now.

"Are you okay?" he asked. "I came looking for Chris and ran into that waitress muttering words I don't think need repeating."

Kelsey could only nod, as she looked back at the pad she held. She didn't dare speak.

"Is something wrong?"

She heard him come closer, felt his presence behind her. Caught the faint scent of his aftershave, of the soap in his clothing.

For a crazy moment she felt an urge to lean back against him. To let his strength hold her up. Then, with the precision of a knife, she remembered what Lorelei had said.

"I'm okay," she managed to say with a calm she didn't feel.

Just as she thought she had mastered her own emotions, his hand lightly feathered her shoulder.

It was so faint, had she not been so aware of him behind her, she might have missed it.

"You don't sound okay," he murmured.

Kelsey took a slow breath angry with the insurgent beating of her heart, the trill that riffled down her neck at his faint touch. What was she? Stupid?

She had just heard Lorelei tell her that her husband had been unfaithful.

And here she was, not ten seconds later, responding to another man. Another man just like her husband.

She lifted her chin and half turned toward him, to tell him to take his hand off her, to leave.

Deep-brown eyes looked with disquiet down at her. He'd pulled his dark eyebrows together in concern.

"Hey, Kelsey," he said softly. "It's okay. She's gone now."

Kelsey had to force herself to look away from the concern in his eyes. It was too dangerous and she was too vulnerable. She could only nod, as she glanced away. "I'll be fine."

"I came to pick up Chris when I saw that waitress come storming out of here," he said, slipping his hand off her shoulder. "Thought maybe you might need some help."

Kelsey looked ahead, directly at the Swain family picture. "No, thanks. I don't need any help."

"Well, I should go get Chris."

Kelsey wanted to tell him no. She wanted to take Chris and run away to some quiet place, just the two of them. No parents, no financial worries. No reminders of Carter.

All week Chris had spoke of nothing else but going to work with Will today. About how when he grew up he was going to run a Cat, just like his dad.

Chris still had his precious memories. She couldn't take that away.

"He's in the kitchen," was all she said.

"Good. I'll bring him home this time. You don't need to come to the job site to get him."

"Okay."

"See you tonight." He tossed her a wave and then left without a second glance, vitality and strength leaving with him.

Kelsey sagged against the desk, her head hanging down. I need time, she thought. Time to work through all this. Time to think, to plan.

But she didn't have it. Her life moved inexorably on, pulling her with it. She felt as if she were stumbling over her feet trying to keep up. Trying to do all the things she was supposed to, trying to deal with the emotions that threatened to overwhelm her at times.

She prayed again and again.

Took a deep breath in then out, as if ridding herself of emotion, of panic and fear.

And what were you thinking of back there? Will reprimanded himself as he walked through the restaurant. Touching her like that. As if it were your right. Well she had made it fairly clear that she was off-limits.

Will shook his head as he rounded the corner by the kitchen. He should know better anyway than to get involved with someone like her. Kelsey represented needs and emotions, commitment and giving.

All the stifling things he strove to avoid. If Will didn't want to be like his father, he wanted even less to end up like his mother. Needing someone left you defenseless.

"Will, you came for me." Chris jumped off the stool he sat perched on and ran toward him, bouncing to a halt beside him. "Can we go now? Right now?"

"Sure, we can."

"Just a minute." The man with the hair net and flour-dusted apron called out to Chris. "Don't forget your muffins."

Chris's eyes went wide, and he hunched his shoulders with exaggerated amusement. "I made some muffins for you and Mom and me. By myself." He dipped one shoulder scrunching up his face. He glanced guiltily at the cook. "Well, Bob helped me." He let go of Will's hand and ran back, taking the bag from Bob, then spun back to Will, energy and enthusiasm emanating from every pore. "We have to give one to my mom," he said, a grin splitting his face. "She likes blueberry the best."

"You go ahead, Chris. I'll wait outside in the truck." Hard not to keep the abrupt tone out of his voice.

"But you have to come with me," Chris insisted. "So she doesn't have to wave goodbye from her window."

"What do you mean, wave goodbye?"

"She watched you yesterday. Out the window,"

Chris continued, puzzlement tingeing his voice at Will's obvious confusion.

"Well, you just go by yourself. I don't think she wants to watch me today. You give her the muffin and I'll wait outside by the truck." Will left the restaurant, confusion warring with his previous declaration of noninvolvement. Just a few moments ago, her cool reaction to him showed him more clearly than ever that she didn't care.

He leaned back against the truck as he waited for Chris, trying very hard not to look at the window of Kelsey's office, trying not to imagine her standing by it, watching him.

A couple of minutes later Chris came bounding out of the restaurant putting an end to this unfamiliar train of thought. Will helped him into the truck and buckled him up.

But as they drove away, he couldn't help glance over to the window of Kelsey's office.

Nor could he stop the funny flip of his heart when he saw a shadow pull back from that same window.

Chapter Six

Kelsey twitched the curtains back from her living room window, as she glanced down the street. It was already five-forty-five. Will and Chris should have been back by now.

Maybe something happened? What if they had an accident?

Kelsey caught the rising panic, slowing it with a few quick breaths.

Since Carter's death she could never completely shake that feeling of vulnerability that could engulf her at the most unexpected times.

If it could happen once, a negative part of her mind always chimed in, it could happen again.

"He will cover you with his feathers, and under his wings you will find refuge; his faithfulness will be your shield and rampart."

How many times hadn't she drawn this Psalm to

herself in the dark days when she was all alone? When her sorrow would threaten to choke her.

God was faithful. God was strength and comfort in life and death.

Now, after what had happened this afternoon, she clung tenaciously to those words. Only God was faithful, she reminded herself as she walked back into the kitchen.

All afternoon, Lorelei's vicious words had twisted through her mind. Hearing those words from a woman Carter had been with was beyond humiliating.

On top of that, it was as if she went through all the same emotions she had the first time she found Connie's letter.

She remembered how little time Carter spent around the house when he was home. How he would avoid fixing all the things that needed doing.

Instead she would wait until Carter was gone off on another job. Then she would phone her father, using Carter's absence as an excuse.

She kept thinking of the insurance money Will spoke of and wondered if there weren't more things about Carter that he knew.

Kelsey walked back to the kitchen, making more noise than usual opening the oven door to check her casserole, trying to keep the silence at bay. The only times she had ever been alone were the days before Chris was born and Carter would be away from home, working on an out-of-town road job. She had hated those empty, lonely evenings when the silence and doubts about Carter pressed in. Then Carter would phone, and for a few moments she was connected to him, important to him. But the phone calls were never long enough and he always had to say goodbye.

And she was left with her loneliness and her doubts again.

Now she knew those doubts were real.

Kelsey slammed the oven door shut, pushing aside the sharp edges of the memory. As soon as she closed the oven door, she heard the thankful sound of Chris's excited voice coming up the walk.

Then the front door crashed open.

"Hi, Mom, we're home," he called out, his little-boy voice filling the house. "You come in, Will," he said and Kelsey heard the murmur of Will's voice replying.

Kelsey unconsciously smoothed her hair, tugged her pale-yellow cardigan straight over the matching tank top. When she'd come home from work, she had hesitated over what to change into. Her usual attire, blue jeans and a sweatshirt, seemed oddly unappealing. Especially when she knew Will would be coming to drop Chris off.

She felt a perverse desire to feel attractive. To salve a pride wounded by Lorelei's assertion that she had spent time with Carter.

So she redid her hair and refreshed her makeup. It wasn't for Will, she told herself.

But now, as she walked to the front door, she felt self-conscious.

Chris sat on the floor of the front entrance tugging on his running shoes, his eyes on Will who knelt down to help him. "We have to tell Mom about the cabin. Tell her that we're gonna stay there one night," he was saying.

Chris saw Kelsey and jumped up, one shoe still on. "Mom, Mom. We went to the cabin again."

"Did you?" Kelsey smiled down at him as he leaned against her. She touched a smudge of dirt on his face. "Sounds like you had a good day. But you should take your other shoe off and then wash up. It's almost supper time."

Chris nodded and walked back to the porch, not noticing the trail of dirt he left in his wake. The other shoe was dealt with quickly, thanks to Will.

"I have to wash my hands," Chris informed him with all the disgust a six-year-old could muster. "Don't go away."

Will smiled lightly. "I'll wait till you come back."

Chris ran off, and she and Will were left alone.

Kelsey crossed her arms and glanced up at him, suddenly self-conscious. She noticed that he wore a clean denim shirt and blue jeans.

"Your shirtsleeves too short for you, too?" she asked, indicating his sleeves rolled up at the forearms.

Will glanced down, then back at her, a smile tugging at one corner of his well-shaped mouth. "Yes. I can seldom buy a shirt off the rack."

"Carter had the same problem. You two must

have been the same height.'' Kelsey caught herself as she spoke the words. Habit, she thought. The habit of a wife who overcompensated for her husband's failings by talking about him as often as possible.

Will's smile faded. "We were both six foot two," he said.

Kelsey was surprised at the change in his tone. Will's drawl was so subtle she wasn't sure if she imagined it or not. It was always there when she mentioned Carter's name and again she wondered what he knew.

"Mom, Mom, I'm done." Chris burst into the room, his hands out for inspection.

"Good job, son."

"Are you going to eat with us, Will?" Chris asked.

"No, I don't think I should."

Chris turned to Kelsey, tugging on her arm. "Can Will stay? Please."

Kelsey noticed once again Will's clean clothes and remembered how, when he would drop Carter off, Carter would always invite him in. Will was always grateful.

Though she didn't know if she was ready to be with him, she also knew it would be downright rude to tell Chris that his invitation to Will would have to be withdrawn.

"Please," she said to Will. "You're welcome to stay."

"See, my mommy wants you to stay," Chris said with pleasure.

"You're not tired of me?" Will asked Chris.

"Of course not." Chris grabbed Will's hand and tugged. "I can show you my room."

In spite of the welter of mixed emotions, Kelsey stifled a quick laugh at the puzzled look on Will's face.

"This is high praise, Will," she assured him. "Chris only lets his very *bestest* friends see his room."

Will caught her gaze, his mouth quirking up in a grin. "Really? I'm honored."

Kelsey felt a renegade response to his smile. Couldn't stop her answering grin.

He held her gaze a moment, a faint frown wrinkling his smooth brow. He looked as if he wanted to say something more, but then Chris tugged on his arm and Will was pulled away.

Kelsey set the table for three. As she placed the salad she had made beside the casserole, she wondered how she was going to work her way through this meal.

She had enough to deal with just living in the present, never mind the past, she reminded herself as she walked to Chris's room.

She paused in the doorway surprised to see Will squatting beside Chris. They were looking over the plans for a spaceship made of building blocks Chris had just received from her parents.

"He's never been able to do that one," Kelsey

said, leaning in the doorway, surprised at the sight. Though Chris was only three when Carter died, she couldn't remember Carter spending much time with Chris.

Will turned a page and nodded. "I'm sure we could figure it out."

"Can we do it now?" Chris asked.

"No, after supper."

Kelsey and Will stopped, aware that each of them had spoken at precisely the same time.

And had said exactly the same words.

We sound like a set of parents, Kelsey thought with a jolt.

"I'm sorry," Will said. "I didn't mean to intrude."

"That's okay," Kelsey assured him hastily, trying to cover up her own startled reaction. "You've had him all day, I'm sure you've had to tell him a time or two what to do." She pushed away from the door, turning away from Will's suddenly enigmatic expression. "It's supper time."

He could do that so well, she thought as she walked back to the kitchen. One minute you thought maybe he was relaxing his guard, letting someone in. Then, as if without warning, the shutters would come down and he was the same evasive man she knew best. For a moment she regretted asking him, wondering how the next hour was going to go.

Thankfully Chris was here, she thought. He would keep the conversational momentum up.

They sat down at the circular wooden table. Chris

between Kelsey and Will. Just before Kelsey was about to pray, Chris held his hand out to Will.

"We always hold hands when we pray," Chris explained. "You have to hold my hand and my mom's hand. Then we make a circle."

"I see," Will said, taking Chris's hand in his. Then he looked across the table at Kelsey. "Orders from the boss," he said lightly, reaching out for her hand.

Kelsey laid hers in his, surprised at the string of calluses on his palm. His long fingers closed over hers and as she lowered her head, she chanced another quick glance at him.

He was studying her, his expression unguarded.

Hungry.

Kelsey tore her gaze away. For a moment there wasn't enough air in the room.

Who was the real Will Dempsey and why did he change so quickly? She wasn't sure if she wanted to know. Her own emotions were in such a flux. All she had once thought important had proven to be so much dust in the wind. There was no center to her life, other than her faith. Other than her son.

She closed her eyes, took a slow breath and sent up yet another quick, silent prayer. She felt Chris squeeze her hand and she felt as if equilibrium had been restored.

Thankful, she began to pray. As she spoke, she connected with her Lord, drew near to Him, drew from His strength. She prayed for the meal, her parents, thanked the Lord for the day and hesitated only a moment, before she prayed, as she always did, that someday they would be able to see Carter again when they met in heaven. This prayer was her way of reminding Chris of his father, of keeping his memory alive.

But when she said Amen, she slipped her hand out of Will's without looking at him, not sure she wanted to see his reaction to her mention of Carter.

"What kind of casserole did you make, Mom?" Chris asked as soon as she was done.

"Shipwreck," Kelsey said, rising to take the lid off the casserole dish. Steam wafted out, aromatic and tantalizing. Kelsey felt suddenly hungry. She hadn't eaten since breakfast.

"It has a funny name, but it tastes good," Chris assured Will. "It gots tomatoes and potatoes and rice and onions and hamburger all cooked together."

"Well, it certainly smells good," Will said.

Kelsey held out her hand for his plate and dared a quick look at him. He was inspecting the casserole, smiling as he did so. He thanked her when she gave him his plate back, heaped with the layers of food.

"You have to have some salad," Kelsey said to Chris, as she sat down.

Chris pouted, but did as he was told.

The meal drifted along, Chris carrying the bulk of the conversation. He told Kelsey about his day. Explained some of the things they had done.

"We saw a big trackhoe putting in..." Chris paused, as he turned to Will. "Those big round things for water. They go under the road."

"Culverts?" Kelsey suggested.

"How did you know?" Chris frowned at her. "How did you know what they were called?"

"I do know a little bit about road construction." Chris looked skeptical.

"It's true," Will affirmed, giving Kelsey a quick grin. "Your mother used to come once in a while to the job site. When your dad was alive."

"But only when you guys were within driving distance," Kelsey returned. "My goodness, that last year and a half your crews were all over the place. I remember coming to the job site once and neither you nor Carter were even there. I don't think I ever told him." She stopped, as she realized what she had said. As she realized, with a flush of shame, the implications of them being gone.

"That was a busy year," he said carefully. There it was again. That pulling back. The smile that slipped a bit when she mentioned Carter's name.

"How many Cats do you have?" Chris piped in, his mind zipping around to the next topic.

From there the talk moved from equipment, to working long hours, to school. Chris was only too glad to tell Will about his teacher and his friends.

As the supper progressed, Will visibly relaxed. In spite of his young age, Chris had the same ability his father did to put people at ease.

"So what do you want to be when you grow up?" Will asked Chris, laying his knife and fork across his plate.

Chris pursed his lips as he considered the ques-

tion. "I wanna be rich. Then I can help my mom."
He grinned at Kelsey who shook her head at his
bluntness.

"And how are you going to get rich?" Kelsey
asked with a grin.

"I'm gonna be like Will." Chris flashed Kelsey
a triumphant look.

"That's good honey." Kelsey slanted a quick
glance toward Will, but he was looking down at his
folded arms.

The silence that hung around the three of them
was punctuated by the ticking of Chris's fork on his
plate as he tried to stab leaves of lettuce.

"Why are you being so quiet?" Chris said suddenly, fiercely concentrating on capturing an elusive
tomato. "I don't have to talk all the time, do I?"

Kelsey couldn't stop the laughter that bubbled up.
"No, you don't, Chris." She gave Will a quick
glance, realizing that she was making more of this
than she had to. She had spent time with Will when
Carter was alive. While not exactly a friend of the
family, she didn't need to treat him like a stranger.
"So, Will. What do you want to be when you grow
up?"

"I guess I'm supposed to say rich," Will said,
smiling now. "But I'll let Chris be rich. I'd sooner
be content."

"And are you?"

He held her gaze, his head tilted carefully to one
side as he considered her question. "Not really."

Kelsey heard the faint note of regret in his voice.

Will gave out so little, she didn't know if she wanted to read more into what he had just said, but she decided to respond to it anyhow. "And how do you propose to go about getting there?"

"I'm not sure."

His quiet admission winged deep into her soul and once again they were silent, each lost in their thoughts.

"Can we have dessert after?" Chris asked as he pushed his plate away. "I'm not hungry after that salad."

"Sounds like a good idea," Kelsey said. "Why don't you get the Bible and we can have devotions?"

Chris jumped off his chair and ran around the counter to the drawer that held their Bible and devotional booklet. He laid it on the table in front of Kelsey and then climbed up on her lap, like he usually did.

Kelsey encircled him with her arms, opening the Bible to where the bookmark was, and began reading from Phillipians 4.

She couldn't help but pause as she came to verse 8.

"'Finally, brothers, whatever is true, whatever is noble, whatever is right, whatever is pure, whatever is lovely, whatever is admirable—if anything is excellent or praiseworthy—think about such things. Whatever you have learned or received or heard from me, or seen in me—put it into practice. And the God of peace will be with you.'"

Kelsey's voice almost wavered at that point. What was true or right or praiseworthy about her marriage with Carter? It seemed like everything she said, pointed back to her broken memories. She cleared her throat and continued. "'I have learned the secret of being content in any and every situation, whether well fed or hungry, whether living in plenty or in want. I can do everything through Him who gives me strength.'"

Kelsey stopped, her finger resting on the words, glancing up at Will. "Well, I guess that's a start for you," she said lightly.

Chris reached for the booklet, and without looking to see Will's reaction, she began reading it, too. It was a practical application of what she had just read. The words were as valid to her as they might be to Will, she thought as she closed the book. She, too, had to learn every day, the lesson of being content in the various circumstances of her life. Had to trust that God's peace would be sufficient for her in the hardships of her life.

She looked over at Will who sat back in his chair, his arms folded over his chest, a thoughtful expression on his face.

"Can I pray, Mom?" Chris asked, leaning back against her shoulder.

"You certainly may," she said, brushing his hair back from his face with one of those unnecessary motherly gestures that communicated so much more.

He grinned up at her then looked back at Will who was watching them, his expression a faint echo of the same hunger she had seen only a few moments ago.

"Do you have anything you want me to pray for?" Chris asked.

Will smiled then, and sitting up, shook his head. "I can't think of anything right now, Chris," he said.

"Not anything?" Chris persisted.

"Well," Will rubbed his cheek with one hand as he considered. "Maybe you could pray for your mom?"

Kelsey's gaze flew to his. What did he mean by that vague request? His eyes held hers and to her chagrin she found she couldn't look away.

"Let's pray, Mom," Chris said, giving her arm a light poke.

Kelsey lowered her head and Chris began his prayer. He prayed for his grandparents who were supposed to be coming home next week. He prayed for Kelsey as per Will, and as always he prayed that his daddy would be happy, as he watched over them.

Then he lifted his head, grinned up at his mom and slipped off her lap.

"Let's go make the spaceship," Chris said, his practical child's nature slipping easily from the sacred to the commonplace.

"Shouldn't we help with the dishes?" Will asked.

Chris screwed up his face. "I don't really like the dishes," he informed Will.

"Know what?" Will said, picking up his plate and stacking it on top of Chris's. "Neither do I. But

I'd sooner eat a home-cooked meal and do dishes, than eat in a restaurant and not do dishes.'' He looked across the table at Kelsey, smiling now. ''Thanks for supper, Kelsey. It was delicious.''

His compliment warmed her. ''You're welcome. And for that bit of praise, I hereby excuse you two from washing up. There's not many.''

''Thanks, Mom,'' Chris jumped up, his fists clenched in victory. ''I'll get the bricks, Will. You wait in the living room.''

''Chris, don't be rude.'' Kelsey was appalled at how easily he ordered Will around.

Chris looked crestfallen. ''Sorry, Will. Can you please wait while I get my bricks?''

''Sure. I'll help your mother in the meantime.''

As Chris left, Kelsey turned to Will. Once again Will had to see Chris acting up and it was embarrassing. ''I'm sorry for his behavior. He's not usually like that. I think he's just excited.''

''It's okay, Kelsey,'' Will said, picking up the dishes he had just stacked. ''He's just a little boy full of spirit. He was really good today. I enjoyed having him around.''

''He didn't talk your ear off?'' Kelsey asked as she picked up the casserole dish, leading the way into the tiny kitchen alcove.

''Actually he was pretty quiet. Loves going to that cabin, though. Likes to pretend we're pioneers and stack firewood.'' Will set the plates down on the counter and paused. ''You've done well with him, Kelsey. Really.''

Again his praise pushed up that curious feeling of goodwill in her.

"Thanks. I love him dearly, but sometimes I feel like I'm not doing enough."

"You said that before. I wouldn't worry about it. You're a good mother, Kelsey Swain."

Just not much of a wife, she thought. She turned away. "Why don't you go help Chris? I can finish up here."

She could feel him hovering, could almost feel his question at her withdrawal. Then, thankfully he left.

Kelsey pulled in a deep breath. She wanted to go out for a long walk, work off the anger, the pain that had twisted in her stomach all day. She wanted to struggle with God. Ask Him why she had to keep finding this out. Why He had brought Will into her life right now, as a reminder of Carter. Will with his questioning eyes, his slightly protective air.

She closed her eyes as if to banish the picture of Will, the emotions he brought out in her. Too long alone, thought Kelsey. That was all it was.

She turned on the taps, filled the sink, squeezed in the soap. All routine motions, but all done with trembling hands.

Please let me get through this, Lord. Please let me just act as I always have.

She wiped the counters, shook the tablecloth out the back door. Little domestic tasks that brought back an air of routine. Of normal.

By the time she was done, she felt more in control. Then she returned to the living room.

Will was sprawled on the living room carpet, his body taking up most of the floor space.

Chris grinned as he looked up at his mother. "We're almost finished."

Kelsey dropped onto the old sofa and smiled back at him. "Great. Grandma and Grandpa will be glad to see it."

When the spaceship was finally completed, Chris spent a few moments pretending he was taking over deep space, on a mission to conquer the universe for Earth.

Half an hour later Kelsey brought out the pie she had made. As they ate it, she forced herself to make small talk with Will. They talked of the weather, how long his job would take. Chris was busy with his spaceship and didn't disturb them. The casual chitchat restored some measure of equilibrium, and Kelsey felt herself relax in Will's presence.

Once the pie was done, it was bedtime for Chris. To her surprise, Chris made no demur.

She sat with him and said his prayers and before she even pulled the sheets around his shoulders, he was drifting off to sleep, still clutching the spaceship.

When Kelsey came back to the living room, Will had cleaned up the plastic bags that held the parts and was putting them in the box. He stood when Kelsey came close.

"Well, I should go," he said, setting the box on

the coffee table. "Once again, thanks for dinner. I really appreciated it."

"You're welcome." She looked at him and in spite of her earlier prayer, found herself wondering again about women in his life. Had he accompanied Carter when he went out? She was pretty sure that women would fall all over him. Will was an attractive man. His reserve made him all the more appealing. Like a challenge.

Kelsey remembered the smile he had given her when she picked up Chris last week at the construction site. What that one small gesture had done to her.

She stopped her thoughts. If she didn't watch herself she was going to end up falling for him. Just like she had for Carter.

He turned and Kelsey followed him to the porch, watching as he put his boots back on, lacing them up. He caught his jacket from the hook and as he slipped it on, he looked at her.

"I can get Chris next Saturday if you want," he offered, holding on to the front panels of his coat.

"Chris has a baseball tournament that day."

"Oh, really? Where?"

"Just here. In Stratton."

Will nodded, his eyes still holding hers.

Kelsey felt a yearning curl up inside her. In spite of everything she knew about Carter, in spite of what she knew about Will, she couldn't stop a very basic need to have someone who cared about her.

Who looked at her the way Will was looking at her now.

"Does he play often?"

"No. It's a pretty low-key league. Cory and her husband, Matthew, coach, if that gives you any indication of the caliber." Kelsey caught the edges of her sleeves with her hands, pulling her sweater around her as Will continued to stand in front of her, making inconsequential talk.

What was he doing? she wondered. What did he want?

He shifted his weight, a slight movement toward her. Kelsey looked away as silence fell between them.

"Thanks again for supper," he said quietly.

Her only response was the faint nod of her head, her eyes still downcast.

Then he turned and left.

Kelsey walked slowly to the window, pulling back the curtain once again. As she did so, she saw Will hesitate and look back at the house, before he got into his truck and drove away.

Chapter Seven

Will parked his truck by his trailer, staring at the dark windows of his fifth wheel. In the clearing, most of the other trailers of the workers were lit up, bright rectangles of golden light creating a feeling of welcome. He could hear a few children's voices from one. From another, came the faint strains of music.

He didn't really want to sit in his trailer all by himself. Not after spending the evening with Kelsey and Chris.

A quick glance over his shoulder showed him that the lights of the office trailer were on. Will got out of his truck and walked over there instead.

The door was slightly open and from the interior Will could hear Drew humming lightly.

"Putting in overtime?" Will asked as he stepped inside.

Drew spun around. "Goodness, Will," he snapped. "You don't need to sneak up on someone like that."

Will walked over to the coffeepot and poured himself a cup. "So, what brings you here this time of the night?"

"Just sending a fax to my dear wife," Drew said, feeding some paper into the machine.

"What could you possibly have to tell her that you haven't said during those forever phone calls of yours?"

"My friend the cynic." Drew shook his head. "Keep that up and there will never be any little Dempseys hanging around here."

"I don't want any little Dempseys hanging around here," Will said, studying the coffee in his cup. "It's no life for kids."

"You seem more than willing to have Kelsey Swain's little boy hanging around here."

Will shrugged the comment away. He didn't want to think about Kelsey and Chris right now. They already occupied a little too much of his thinking time. "I'm just doing his mother a favor, that's all."

"I see."

Will sighed. Drew could say more in two words than most people could in a paragraph.

"Look, Drew. The reason I bring Chris here is otherwise the poor kid has to hang around that restaurant all day because his mother has to work there while Kelsey's parents, who technically own the restaurant, are off on some vacation, leaving her all alone to handle everything," he stopped, hearing the anger seep into his voice. He took a slow breath. Then another. Keep a lid on it Dempsey, he reminded himself.

Drew watched him. Silent.

"What's the matter?" Will asked.

"You seem a little heated. Why should you care?"

"Drop it, Drew."

Drew shook his head slowly. "I don't know. I think something's going on here."

"Nothing is."

Drew was silent a moment. "I beg to differ. We've known each other awhile, Will...."

"This sounds like one of your 'so this gives me the right to boss you around' speeches." Will leaned farther back into his chair. With Drew it was usually better to let him ramble on. Let him feel like he was giving you fatherly advice. Once he was done, then Will could leave.

"You've always been a pretty cool customer, Will," Drew replied. "No matter how bad things are you always project this aura of calm. I've seen guys yell and scream, and you come into the scene and everyone just kind of tones down. I've been around you when things aren't going well. You manage to lower the tension level, just by being there. I've envied that many times. But I've also watched your girlfriends, tears pouring down their cheeks as they try to get through that cool reserve, and you just calmly hand them a hanky."

Will sighed. "Point?"

"My point, my dear friend, is that I've seldom seen you lose that control you pride yourself on. But since you've been around this Kelsey, you are starting to show a few vestiges of normal. I see a few emotions creeping in, like just a moment ago. And for that I am thankful."

"And what is normal?" Will finished off the rest of his coffee, annoyance with his friend the chief emotion he was feeling now. He should have gone to his trailer instead of being subjected to yet another analysis of his life. "Yelling because things don't go right? Screaming at someone who only gets more clumsy when you do that? Getting all emotional because some woman is trying to manipulate you with her tears?"

"Women don't cry on purpose, Will."

"Some do."

"Some don't."

Will shrugged. "That's a draw."

"C'mon, Will. Hasn't the sight of a woman crying ever melted your heart?"

Will ran his finger around the rim of his cup as Drew's question brought up a recent memory.

Of Kelsey standing by the grave of a man that she loved, her head bowed. She was crying over a man who didn't deserve her tears. Under most circumstances he would think she was a fool.

But Kelsey's sorrow had brought out a depth of emotion he had never felt before.

Drew read more into his momentary reticence

than Will wanted him to. Will knew this conversation was going nowhere. Well, actually, it was going the same place Drew seemed to head every conversation.

Drew just figured that Will needed a woman. A wife. Marriage.

In spite of his changing feelings for Kelsey Swain, the thought frightened him. Marriage meant losing yourself, losing your self-respect. His mother was a prime example of that. Always giving in to his father, slowly subverting her own will and desires until she became whatever his father wanted her to be.

"So I see the mighty Will does have a few weak spots," Drew said.

"Of course I have weak spots," Will replied, feeling testy. "You make me sound like I have a heart of stone."

"I know better than that, Will."

Will looked up to see his friend looking at him with a measure of sorrow.

"I know why you are the way you are," Drew said, his voice holding a note of sympathy. "I know what your father was like. But I also know that your admirable self-control can be intimidating to people. It keeps them away. And I see you getting lonelier and lonelier."

"Why do you seem to think that marriage is going to solve my problems?"

"I'm not just talking about marriage. I'm also talking about your faith life."

Will shrugged. He didn't feel like listening to Drew's reminders of where he should be going. Of how he should be living. He should just get up and leave.

But he couldn't.

Because the part of him that could easily recall his grandmother's teachings, the part of him that recognized a Creator and a need to be reconciled to Him, told him to sit and listen.

"And how am I going to repair that leaky vessel?" Will asked with a quiet smile.

"I've taken my family to a really nice church in Stratton. I'm not going this Sunday, though."

Will only nodded.

"I know that Kelsey goes there, too."

Will paused at the entrance to the church building, unconsciously fiddled with his tie and wondered once again what he hoped to gain by going inside.

Peace? Absolution?

Get Drew off his back?

Maybe catch another glimpse of Kelsey?

He smoothed a hand over his hair as if erasing the questions. He was here and figured he may as well see it through. He tugged his coat straight and pulled on the door.

Once inside, he heard the faint notes of a piano playing a hymn, voices and laughter.

"Good morning."

He turned to face a cheerful woman whose bright-red lips perfectly matched the shade of her dress.

She held out a couple of pieces of paper flashing him a welcoming smile. "So glad you could come to our service," she said.

He took the papers, and returned the smile. But the woman only blinked and wouldn't release the papers. For a moment he wondered if he had done something wrong.

Then he felt a hand on his shoulder and he glanced sideways to face Kelsey's friend, Cory. Her brown eyes fairly sparkled. "You have to be careful how you bestow that charming smile of yours," she said quietly. "It can be lethal." To the woman who had by now recovered, Cory said, "Morning Mrs. Phipps. This is Will Dempsey. He's in charge of that highway job they're doing north of Stratton."

Mrs. Phipps carefully smoothed her perfectly coiffed hair and gave Will another smile. "Welcome to Stratton, Mr. Dempsey. I hope you enjoy it here."

"I hope so, too," he said. Then he turned to Cory who stood, grin firmly in place, beside a tall brown-haired man dressed in an immaculately cut navy suit.

"Hello again, Cory," Will said.

"Wow. He remembers names. I'm impressed." She turned to the man beside her, a look of pride suffusing her face. "And this is my husband, Matthew. Matthew, I'd like to introduce Will Dempsey."

"Welcome to Stratton," Matthew said, taking Will's hand.

Will was about to murmur some polite reply,

when the doors of the foyer opened again letting in a shaft of light.

And Kelsey.

He couldn't stop the shift in his stance so he could see her better, couldn't stop himself from tugging on his tie, a gesture reminiscent of Mrs. Phipps preening just a few moments ago.

Kelsey was half-turned, urging her son into the foyer.

"C'mon, Chris. You can talk to your friends after church." She reached behind her, and gently ushered him in.

Will couldn't stop watching as Kelsey smoothed Chris's hair back from his face, straightened the collar of his shirt and then gently touched the corner of his mouth. "There. That's my handsome boy," she said as Chris smiled.

Another couple came through the doors and Kelsey, looking up from Chris, greeted them warmly as well.

She did that so easily, thought Will, watching as Kelsey rested a hand on the woman's arm, inquired after the husband's health. That connection she made so quickly with others. All done with a light hand, a quick smile.

"She's good, isn't she?" Cory murmured beside him.

Will gave a start. He had forgotten all about Cory.

"I'm sorry," he said, turning back to her. "What did you say?"

Cory looked up at him and winked. "Just pointing

out a few of my dear friend's virtues. It's amazing how people warm up to her," she said, meaning-fully.

"And it's amazing how much you can talk," Matthew interjected, tugging on his wife's arm. "Enjoy the service," he said to Will. He looked down at Cory with an admonishing look. She wrinkled her nose up at him, tucked her arm through his and Will was forgotten.

For a moment Will envied them. They looked so happy. Complete.

He shook his head. Outward appearances, he reminded himself.

"Will. Hi." Chris called out his name and Will turned back to Kelsey and her son.

Chris pulled free from his mother's hand and ran toward him, his smile welcoming. "You never been here before," he stated as if Will might not be aware of that fact. He turned, calling out to Kelsey, "Mommy, Will is here."

Kelsey's advance was more controlled than her son's, as was her smile.

"I'm glad you could make it," she stated, clasping her hands in front of her. Her gray suit gave her a more austere air than the jeans and sweater set she wore last night. Made her less approachable.

He didn't like it.

"I thought I would take the day off," he explained, hoping he sounded more offhand than he felt. "See if I can remember some of the old songs."

"If you're looking for 'Amazing Grace,' you

might have to come to quite a few services," Kelsey said. "We try to mix some contemporary songs in with the older hymns."

"I'm looking forward to it, then."

"And I'm glad to hear that." She hesitated, then caught Chris by the hand. "We should find a place to sit, Chris."

"Are you going to sit with us, Will?" Chris piped up, fairly dancing beside them with suppressed excitement. "We always sit with my grandma and grandpa, but they're not here today."

"Mr. Dempsey might want to sit on his own," Kelsey said, still avoiding Will's gaze.

"I think I can find a place, Chris," Will said, giving Kelsey an out.

But just before she entered the sanctuary, Kelsey cast him a sideways look that sent a riffle of response through him.

If only Drew could see him now, Will thought, slightly irritated with how easily Kelsey could get a rise out of him.

Will waited until Kelsey sat down, then allowed the usher to seat him. Unfortunately for both of them, the usher put him directly across the aisle from Kelsey. He wasn't going to look, he told himself, but it was as if an irresistible force pulled on him.

He finally gave her a quick glance, surprised to see her suddenly avert her head.

The service began with a few announcements delivered in a dull monotone by a less than enthusiastic council member. Will crossed his arms and settled back. So far it was much like the church services his grandmother used to take him to.

Then a group came to the front. A couple of boys picked up guitars, a young girl seated herself behind the drums, another stood behind an electric piano.

At the same time a screen came down from the ceiling, an overhead projector went on and the group broke into the loud, vibrant chords of a song Will had never heard sung in any church service he had ever attended.

The entire congregation, surged to their feet and began to sing along. Will got up, bemused at the air that permeated the congregation.

Some people clapped along.

Kelsey was one of them.

Will tried to sing along, but found his eyes straying again and again to the animated woman across the aisle from him. She smiled as she sang, totally at ease.

He turned back to the words on the screen, reading without singing. The song spoke of a river of God's love, flowing and washing. He felt an air of excitement permeate the congregation, an air of unrestrained happiness.

The song segued into another, then another as the enthusiasm flowed around him, captivating and beckoning. He felt the tug of a smile, felt his heart lift as if he sensed, through the singing, the love that God was holding out to him.

Then, to his disappointment, as quickly as the

song started it was done. He took a slow breath, surprised at what had come over him. For a moment he felt as if feelings were washing over him, pulling him along in that river of love.

Out of control.

He sat down, shaken by what he had just experienced. They were just songs, but they had moved him more than any song he had sung before.

He wanted to look at Kelsey again. To share with her what he had just experienced, but when he looked over she was busy with Chris.

The minister got up and welcomed everyone to the service. He then invited the congregation to read along with him in the Bible. The passage he read spoke of God's law and how we always fall short of fulfilling the requirements of the law.

"Jesus told us the fulfilling of the law is to love God above all else and your neighbor as yourself," the minister concluded, closing his Bible.

"Easy words to say, hard to do. *Love* is one of the most misused words in the English language, it is treated with scorn and with derision. It is used to manipulate and to bend. Yet it remains a word full of the power of God."

What the minister said so closely echoed what Will had always felt about the word *love*.

His father had told his mother he loved her countless times.

Carter had said he loved Kelsey. But would a man who loved his wife leave her the way he had? Without money, without any way of supporting herself?

The only true example of love he had seen in his life was his grandmother's love for him. Drew's love for his family.

He looked sidelong at Kelsey. And the love Kelsey had for her son.

Kelsey looked straight ahead as she listened to the minister, a smile teasing the soft line of her lips. And Will knew he was seeing yet another kind of love.

The minister spoke for a while longer and Will listened attentively, his words challenging and disconcerting at the same time. All too soon, though, the minister was done and announced another song.

This time the piano and organ started up with a burst of harmony.

Will looked down at the books in the rack in front of him wondering which one he was supposed to use. He glanced at his neighbor this time and picked out the same book and found the number. This song was familiar. It was one his grandmother used to sing.

As he looked over the words, it was as if he could hear her slightly off-key voice singing even now.

"'Have thine own way, Lord.'" The congregation sang the old-fashioned song, slowly, reverently, but Will couldn't join in. He couldn't do what the song said. Give over, let go. Let God mold and make him.

Control was what he had striven for so many years. Control of his life, control of his destiny, his own vision. Control of his emotions.

Once again he found himself looking over at Kelsey who pointed out the words to Chris as they sang. Teaching her child by word and example. Carrying on a tradition that had been given to her by her parents.

Kelsey turned her head slowly, as if sensing his gaze. She held his eyes for a moment, then lowered them, turning away. Her hair fell across her face, obscuring it from Will's view and she didn't push it away.

Hiding.

As Will looked ahead again he felt an unfamiliar confusion grip him. He knew what was happening and how dangerous it could be. The glances that skittered away at the last moment. The hesitant probing.

All signs of a quickening interest that his practical side knew he should not encourage in either himself or her. Not when he knew that soon he had to leave.

And not when the shadow of Carter hung so darkly between them.

He glanced sidelong again. Then she turned her head, her eyes met his and that disconcerting yearning returned.

The same yearning that brought him here.

Chapter Eight

"How about consolidating the line of credit and the mortgage and extending the term?" Kelsey leaned her forehead on her hands as she listened to their banker tell her what she already knew she would hear. "We've got a little bit of room left. I know we do," she said, struggling to keep her tone impersonal.

"Okay. I'll come in next week with my father and we can figure out a solution to this. Thanks." Kelsey hung up, her chair creaking as she sat back.

It had taken a couple of weeks, but by dint of pushing and displaying a measure of overconfidence, she had elicited a momentary reprieve from the relentlessness of their bank account.

Actually all it would do was extend the misery. The best solution was putting the restaurant up for sale. And what chance did they have to sell it in such a small town?

If it didn't sell...

Kelsey pushed that insidious worry aside. It didn't take much imagination to see her parents destitute and Kelsey trying to support them.

After coming back from their holiday, her father was supposed to come to the restaurant today. But her mother just phoned to tell her that Bill Hartley had a severe migraine, which meant she wouldn't see him here for a couple more days. Her father's migraines were debilitating, and Kelsey felt the pressure of one more burden on her shoulders.

She wished she was ten years old and could indulge in a good crying jag, as if that would do any good.

She wished she could just get up and walk away from this place as Cory had suggested numerous times but she knew it had never been an option.

She wished a hero would come swooping into her life to rescue her.

"While you're at it, why don't you wish you could spin straw into gold," she muttered, pulling open the folder and dropping into her chair. It was about as feasible. There were no heroes in life.

The phone rang again, and Kelsey was tempted to ignore it. No good news ever came over the phone.

But she could no more ignore the phone than she could walk away from the restaurant. She reached across the desk and snagged the phone off the hook. "Hartley's Restaurant, Kelsey here," she said shortly, frowning at a loan agreement that was twenty years old.

"Did I catch you at a bad time?"

Kelsey felt a momentary shock at the sound of Will's deep tones. She hadn't seen him for a week and a half. He hadn't come to the restaurant. Last Saturday Chris had started playing baseball so Will hadn't picked him up. Nor had Will been in church on the following Sunday.

Kelsey had told herself it was all for the good. Told herself that she should be wiser than to become involved with another man.

But now, after a lapse of ten days, she was just as twittery at the sound of his voice as any girl with her first crush.

She swallowed and took a slow breath. Settle down, girl. Just another guy, she reminded herself. Carter's partner.

"Not really," she said, "Just doing some book work."

"With a calculator that doesn't work?"

His light joke caught her by surprise, and for a moment she didn't speak. In the background Kelsey could hear the faint roar of equipment, and she easily pictured him sitting in his truck.

"No. With a banker that won't work," she replied.

"I had one of those once."

Kelsey leaned back in her chair, her elbows tucked close against her, his unexpected give-and-take surprising her.

"So what did you do with him?" she asked, unable to resist the temptation of prolonging the conversation that was about nothing, yet everything. She felt like a Ping-Pong ball. Her head said stay away, but her lonely heart, hurting from Carter's duplicity seemed to lean toward this man from her past. This man who, if she were to be honest, had always held a dangerous appeal.

"Him was a her. And I didn't do anything. Just made some money that year. That helped."

Kelsey smiled a humorless smile. "That's where things fall apart for me. I don't foresee that happening."

Silence and she wondered if she had sounded too whiny.

"So what are you up to now?" she asked.

"Just doing some phoning." Another beat of silence from him. "And I was wondering if you were busy on Friday night."

Kelsey's heart did that silly little flop again. "Why do you want to know?"

"I'd like to take you out for dinner. A way of saying thanks for having me over on Saturday."

Not a good idea, her head told her.

How long had it been since she had gone out on a date, her heart asked her?

You have Chris to think of, she thought. You have enough to do. You don't have the emotional strength to deal with this man. He's far too attractive.

"It was just a casserole, Will. Nothing special,"

she answered quickly, trying to find a gracious way to decline.

"Well, it was special to me."

His words hung in the disembodied space that telephones create as she tried not to read more into his comment than absolute face value.

"I haven't spent time with a family for a long time," he continued. "I appreciated it. I'd like to return the favor. Besides—" he paused a moment "—I, uh, have some business I would like to discuss with you."

"What business?" Kelsey asked, puzzled.

"That's why I want to take you out. So I can talk about it there."

Kelsey frowned, not sure how to handle this. "Okay." If it was business, it should be okay. Then it wasn't technically a date, was it? And she wasn't being a foolish woman, unable to learn her lessons.

"Good, when can I pick you up on Friday?"

Kelsey calculated, then made a quick decision. "Why don't I meet you there?" She was still uncomfortable around him. Having her own transportation would give her a chance to leave when she chose to.

And it would make it look like less of a date.

"I don't like that idea at all."

She knew he would protest, but she also knew that she needed to hold her ground. "It just works out better for me. I insist."

He sighed. "Okay. I'll see you at seven at the Prairie Inn then."

"Good." She could sense his displeasure, but knew that having her own vehicle would give her the space she needed around him and would give her a measure of independence. "See you then."

She rung off and laid the phone down. She couldn't stop the faint lift of her heart at the thought of being with Will then shook her head at her reaction.

"He said he had business to discuss," she reminded herself, as if saying the words aloud would make them real.

She turned and looked at the picture of Carter. She had meant to take it down, but for Chris's sake, decided to keep it hanging.

In spite of what Lorelei had told her, her anger had abated. Yet she still struggled with her own ignorance of what Carter had been doing. She just didn't know how she could have been so wrong about someone. So completely taken in. She had better be sure the same thing didn't happen with her and Will Dempsey. She was a lonely widow woman. The perfect cliché.

Please, Lord, I want to be wise about this, she prayed. *Help me to keep my head and heart connected. Help me to recognize my priorities.*

"Will Dempsey?" Bill Hartley looked up from his newspaper, frowning at his daughter. "What is with this guy?"

Kelsey handed her mother a cartoon video,

frowned at her son and then looked back at her father. "What do you mean?"

Bill lowered the paper, frown still intact. "I hear from Chris that he's been coming to your home. You've been seeing him and now you've got a date with him."

"Dad, I know you thought the world of Carter, but he's been dead for three years now." Her father's surprising animosity put Kelsey on the defensive. "Surely I should be dating other men." Though this wasn't a date, her mind mocked her.

"I wish it was other men. Why him?"

"You hardly know him. Why not him?"

Bill gave his newspaper a shake as his frown deepened. "I know enough of him. He's not to be trusted."

Neither was Carter, but her Dad doted on Carter. Always said he was the son he never had.

"He's an old friend, Dad. Carter trusted him, I'm sure."

Her father just frowned.

"You look just lovely," Donita said, patting her daughter on the shoulder.

"Thanks, Mom." Kelsey had dithered for most of the afternoon, trying to choose something that wouldn't send the wrong message. She had finally settled on a simple sheath in a soft ivory tone. A chiffon overblouse in pale peach softened its clean lines.

"I'm sure you'll have a fine time," Kelsey's

mother said with what sounded like a forced jocularity as she tucked a stray curl behind Kelsey's ear.

Donita's comment didn't sound much more encouraging than her father's as Kelsey wondered where this veiled antipathy came from.

If they were this opposed to Will, she wondered how they would react if they knew the truth about Carter.

She pushed that thought aside. In time she might tell them, but not until Chris was old enough to handle the truth.

She snagged her son's arm as he hurtled past and warned him to settle down. He gave her a quick kiss and then went to sit by his grandfather.

Kelsey smiled at the sight, thankful once again for her parents and the security they had given her. Thankful for the loving home she had grown up in.

Once again, she felt a pang, thinking about Chris, wondering if she would ever dare let herself fall in love again.

With a quick wave to her parents, Kelsey left and soon was getting out of the car in the parking lot of the Prairie Inn, clutching her coat against the cool evening air.

"If things go really bad, I could always work here," she said to herself, slightly jealous of the new exterior they had just put on.

Except she knew the boss of the Prairie Inn. She also knew that very few people could work with him.

Kelsey glanced at her watch as she walked to the

large smoked-glass doors of the front lobby. Still on time.

Once inside, the hostess recognized her immediately. "Just hang up your coat, Kelsey, and I'll show you to your table. Will Dempsey is here already."

"Thanks, Janelle." As Kelsey hung up her jacket, she glanced around, taking in the secluded atmosphere of the Prairie Inn. She had been here a couple of times before and always had to suppress a moment's envy at the decor, the subdued elegance. Her restaurant catered to a different crowd, and she enjoyed the ambience, but a small part of her still hankered after this.

Will had chosen a table in the very back of the dining room, in the most insular corner. In spite of her cool attitude, Kelsey couldn't stop the insurgent beating of her heart at the sight of Will's dark hair, the banked glow in his eyes. Just a casual meeting with an old friend of the family, she reminded herself, rubbing her fingers together at her side, fidgeting with her overblouse.

He got up as they approached, his curt nod simultaneously dismissing and thanking an obviously smitten Janelle.

"You're early," he said quietly as he pulled out a chair for her.

"You're even earlier," she replied, avoiding his gaze.

Tonight he wore a dark-gray suit and a white shirt cinched with a black tie. All combined to create a veneer of civilization at odds with the Will Dempsey she had seen just last week. If anything it made her feel even more self-conscious around him.

This was looking less and less casual all the time, she thought, fiddling unnecessarily with the collar of her overblouse. She should have suggested he thank her with a dinner at her restaurant.

"Would you like an appetizer?" he asked as he settled down across the table from her.

She shook her head.

"Then you may as well figure out what you want to order," Will said.

Kelsey took a slow breath, trying to steady the erratic tempo of her heart. This was foolish, she thought. They had a whole evening ahead of them and already she was wondering at the wisdom of her decision.

She had never been alone with him.

She held up the menu like a shield between them as she forced herself to act like a mature adult and not a giddy teenager. He was just Will Dempsey. She'd seen him sprawled on her living room floor playing with her son's blocks.

The memory made her smile. Made her relax.

"And how was work this week?" She looked directly at him, compelling herself to hold his steady gaze.

"Good. I've only had to fire one man."

Kelsey thought of her own experience. She looked down at his hands as he toyed with a fork, suppressing a shiver at the memory both of Lorelei's words and of his supportive touch later.

"I suppose you're better at it than me," she said with a light laugh, striving to cover up her awareness of this man.

"It's never easy." He balanced the fork in his hands. "I would sometimes get Carter to do it." He stopped, the name slicing through the air between them. He paused, looking down a moment. "I'm sorry."

Kelsey bit her lip, experiencing a touch of sorrow and confusion. In spite of what Carter did to her, he was Will's friend.

She leaned forward, reaching out to him and covered his warm hand with her own. "I keep forgetting you must miss him, too."

Will held her gaze, his head canted slightly to one side. His mouth curved in a faint smile as his fingers shifted and captured hers. "I do. At times."

Will's deep eyes met hers and Kelsey felt a moment of connection that whispered along her senses as support changed to something completely different. She held his gaze, forced herself to keep her hand on his even as awareness arced between them.

"Carter talked about you often," she continued. "How he liked working with you."

Will stroked his fingers over her hand, but said nothing.

Kelsey's breath slipped free at his light touch. She waited a moment, ostensibly to show him that she was undisturbed by him then withdrew, uncomfortable and yet unable to stop the quick stab of anticipation.

"I remember you told Chris he was a good worker." She didn't want to talk about Carter. She didn't want to even think about him, but right now she used him as a shield. In spite of her determination to keep a distance from Will, she found herself drawn to him from the moment she sat down at the table.

"He was." Will looked serious again.

Kelsey leaned back, watching him, wondering what he was thinking about. Wondering what secrets of Carter's he knew.

The waiter came and took their order, and they were alone again.

Will rubbed his chin with his forefinger, his dark eyes on her. In the subdued light, he looked even more enigmatic than usual.

She took a deep breath, resolved to find out more about this man whom she knew so little about. Maybe once that happened some of the tension she always felt around him would ease. "Carter told me that you inherited your business from your father," she said, folding and unfolding the cloth napkin in front of her. "You mustn't have been very old when that happened."

Will shook his head, leaning back again in his chair. "I was about twenty-five when my father died. But I had already been working with him for ten years before that."

"So you were fifteen when you started working?"

Will nodded. "My father didn't think school was

important." He smiled, but it was without humor. "My mother home-schooled me, but work slowly took the place of the schooling. I tried to keep it up in the evenings, but I was too tired."

Kelsey heard the regret in his voice and for the first time since she met him, wondered at what his home life was like. Wondered if he would tell her.

"Twenty-five is quite young to take over that kind of responsibility. How did you manage?"

"Asked a lot of questions, listened to a lot of advice and then made up my own mind." He tilted a shoulder as if downplaying what he had done. "At any one time in my life I ran Cat, loader, crawler tractor, backhoe, earthmover. Drew was a good foreman for my father. He helped me out a lot. In a number of ways," he added softly.

"In what ways?" Kelsey prompted, curious by this slight revelation from him.

"Drew showed me how to be a boss. How to earn respect. I'm still learning from him."

Kelsey sensed a deeper meaning in what he said. "So why didn't he want to be your partner instead of Carter?"

"Drew likes to pick and choose what he does. He's very fussy about how much family time he gets." An enigmatic smile played around his mouth. "He always tells me that his family is a gift from God that he has to nurture. If his work interferes with that, then the work goes."

Kelsey felt another flutter in response to Will's

smile. "And do you agree with him?" she said quickly, trying to cover her response.

"In part." Will looked directly at her now, his dark gaze riveting her. "I have quite a minimal family."

"Is your mother still alive?"

"She lived with my grandmother in Dawson Creek up until her death a couple of years ago. I still go see my grandmother once in a while. If I'm not too far away."

"No siblings?"

Will shook his head. "From what my mother tells me, she hadn't counted on even having me." He shrugged, as if discounting the harshness of what he had just said.

Kelsey pleated the napkin carefully, searching for the right words, sensing that he had just given her a faint glimpse of things he didn't tell too many others.

She glanced up at him, hoping she could make herself clear. "I think it's sad when a child grows up knowing that they weren't supposed to be 'here,'" she said with slight emphasis on the final word.

She was rewarded with another glimmer of a smile.

"You're very observant," he said succinctly.

Kelsey sensed that subject was closed for now. But in spite of that minor setback, she cast about for something else to talk about, her curiosity piqued by the little bit he had opened up to her.

She wanted to tell him a joke, just for the pleasure of seeing his face soften. Of seeing his smile transform the austere planes of his face, drawing her in. She pulled her thoughts up short and returned to the subject they had been discussing. "You said your grandmother is still alive?"

Will nodded, pulling closer to the table, leaning his elbows on it. "My mother's mother. Jean Payne. She's a wonderful person."

For the first time since she had met him, Kelsey heard genuine warmth in Will's voice, saw his eyes soften and for some unfathomable reason, was jealous of an older lady she had never met.

"She pretty special?"

"Her home was sanctuary for me when I was growing up. We were on the road a lot with my dad's business. My mom always came along so that meant I came along. We lived in small places—trailers, motel rooms. Hard to get away from each other." He was silent a moment and Kelsey remembered his oblique comment about his parents' marriage. "We'd come back to Dawson Creek over the winter season, and I'd often take off to Grandma Jean's. My parents didn't really care. I sometimes spent two weeks there before they would come and get me." He shrugged, as if dismissing the memory.

Kelsey's warm heart softened even more as she imagined Will as a young boy, not even being missed by his parents.

"What is your grandmother like?"

"Smart. Kind. Wise." Another smile flitted

across his face. He rubbed his chin with his index finger as he looked past her, as if to another place. "She would take me to church. Tell me to listen, to absorb whatever part of God I heard or experienced and save it against the days I would need Him."

"And did you?"

Will laughed shortly, a humorless laugh. "I tried. But I didn't go to church enough and the parts I saw of God, I used up very quickly. My parents never went to church, nor did they encourage anything remotely connected to church. When I turned twelve, we moved away from Dawson Creek. I never really connected with another Christian until..." he stopped, laughing again.

"Until what?" Kelsey prompted, her heart warming to this side of Will. She remembered Sunday, how he seemed to absorb everything that went on in church. As if taking his grandmother's advice.

He looked at her again, his eyes softer, the firmness gone from his features.

Kelsey swallowed, suddenly breathless at the change in him. At his undeniable appeal. At the way his eyes held hers, drawing her in.

"Until I met you," he said quietly.

Silly that four simple words from Will could create this breathlessness, this feeling that any movement on her part would break something fragile.

Their eyes caught and as they held, everything else around them, the subdued chatter of the other patrons, the faint tinkling of crystal, faded away until there was only Will and her.

Finally Kelsey blinked, and looked away, breaking the insidious connection, pulling herself back into the here and now. This was dangerous, she thought, wondering how she was going to make it through the rest of the evening.

"What do you mean?" she asked, surprised at the slightly breathless tone of her voice.

"I remember the first time I heard you pray," Will continued, his voice even. "Carter had invited me over for supper. You had that same naturalness that my grandmother had. That same conversational way of talking with God. I missed it more than I realized."

"Did you go to church when you were away from home?"

"No. I didn't know what I believed. I heard one thing, saw another." He shrugged again. "What about you? You seem to have grown up in a fairly stable environment."

"Yes, I have," Kelsey said. "I've been very blessed. My parents' home has been a solid place for me, a place where God was served with heart, soul and mind."

"And you don't have any brothers or sisters, either?"

"No. Just me. My mother had always wanted a dozen kids, but I was all they got." Kelsey grinned back at him. "So we are both only children."

"And you've lived in Stratton all your life?"

"Yes."

Will tilted his head, as if to understand her better.

"Haven't you ever wanted to travel? To see other places?"

"Maybe. Sometimes." Kelsey ran her finger along the edge of the starched napkin. "I dreamed at times of visiting Paris. Trying out some of the restaurants there. French cuisine and all that. Carter talked about going, but it never happened. There never was enough money."

She glanced up at Will, disappointed to see his habitual enigmatic expression back.

"Do you miss him still?"

"You asked me that already," she said quietly, wondering how to tell him and be true to herself. "I missed him at first. I missed him so bad it was like an ache that wouldn't go away. I felt that God had cheated us, had taken away something that I had been yearning for ever since I was little." She laughed lightly.

"And what was that?"

Kelsey felt a flush of embarrassment tinge her cheeks, but in the light of how he had opened up to her, decided to carry on. "I've always been a silly romantic. I used to read fairy stories. Still enjoy them once in a while. But when I was younger, I used to dream that a hero would come sweeping into Stratton to take me away." She lifted her shoulder self-consciously.

"Then Carter came into your restaurant and your life."

Kelsey laughed lightly. "Yes." But Carter had proven to be a knave, rather than a hero.

She looked up at him, her mind easily bringing back that day when she first met them. But somehow, the image of Carter kept fading away. Instead she could more easily recall the picture of Will.

The way his dark eyes followed her.

She tore her gaze away, her heart pounding as the memory blazed into her mind. And behind it the realization she had always pushed aside whenever she thought of Will.

That her first memory of him had always been stronger than her first memory of Carter. That when she saw the two of them together, it was Will whom she couldn't keep her eyes from.

It was Will to whom she had been attracted at first.

She folded her now cold hands on her lap, her heart stuttering as memory after memory layered themselves in her mind.

Will at their wedding, Will sitting in their home. *No, Lord. This is all wrong. I can't be falling in love with him. I can't do this again.*

Chapter Nine

When the waiter brought their order, Will felt a moment's relief.

Each time Kelsey brought up Carter's name, each time she spoke about him as if Carter had been the answer to all her dreams, he felt an inexplicable burst of jealousy followed by anger. How could she have been so blind?

And as always, he had to resist the temptation to tell her what he knew. It wouldn't change anything for either of them. It was past.

The waiter set out their food. Steak for Will, fajitas for Kelsey. They thanked him, and as he withdrew, Kelsey hesitated a moment, then lowered her head in prayer.

Will knew he shouldn't be watching her as she prayed. For in this moment, with her head bowed, her eyes closed, she was defenseless.

But he couldn't look away.

The frown that had furrowed her brow just a moment before faded away, her soft mouth curved in a delicate smile as her expression exuded a peace that he suddenly yearned for.

Then, after a moment's pause, he lowered his own head. He didn't know exactly why he did it. Part of it may have been a response to her own prayer. Part of it was a hearkening back to when he was a young boy, staying with his grandmother. The only person who had taught him to pray.

He felt his mind go blank, remembered vague snatches of half-remembered prayers. *Please, Lord, bless this food....* He paused, trying to remember the rest of the prayer. But it wouldn't come.

Instead he remembered Kelsey's easy conversational tone. But he didn't know what to pray for other than patience and an answer to the questions that plagued him, a filling of the emptiness that grew each year.

He recalled what the minister spoke of on Sunday and asked that he be shown the right thing to do.

When he raised his head, Kelsey was already done. Relieved, he unfolded his own napkin and laid it carefully on his lap, glancing down at the food in front of him. The aroma of the steak, grilled to a sizzling perfection, made his mouth water.

He glanced across at Kelsey, disconcerted to see her studying him.

When he first thought of this ''date'' he had a number of objectives in mind. The main one, he told himself, was to find a diplomatic way to discharge the obligation he had felt since he first found out about Carter canceling the life insurance policy. The "business" he had obliquely referred to.

The other, was not so clearly formed. Merely a faint hope that spending time with her would diminish the fascination she held for him.

It wasn't working.

"You said you were home-schooled," Kelsey said, arranging the various bowls that came with her meal. She glanced up at him with a smile, obviously ready to talk about something else. "Did you go to a regular school at all?"

Will picked up his own fork and toyed with his vegetables while he considered her question, thankful for the return to a more casual give-and-take.

"If we were in a place long enough, I would attend school," he said finally, feeling as if he had to apologize for his lack of education. "But more often than not, we moved around."

"So, no high school experiences? No fighting with locker combinations, no skipping classes, stealing French fries from someone else's plate in the cafeteria?"

Will couldn't help but laugh at her mischievous grin.

"I did go to high school for a couple of semesters one year when dad was short of work. But not long enough to get my picture in any yearbook." He cut off a piece of steak and ate, watching Kelsey as he did.

He didn't want to talk about his past anymore. It sounded dysfunctional and for some curious reason he didn't want Kelsey to think less of him for it.

Kelsey forked a few pieces of chicken, dripping with sauce onto her tortilla.

"That's a messy meal," he commented, changing the subject.

She grinned up at him.

"I thought of that after I ordered. And here I was hoping to impress you with my terribly ladylike manners." She shook her head and finished preparing her fajita. Then with another grin that did nothing for his equilibrium, she leaned forward and took a bite.

Some juice dripped out of the tortilla and down one side of her mouth, but her hands were full and she couldn't stop it soon enough. Will grabbed his napkin and quickly touched it to her cheek, his other hand catching her chin. He paused as once again their eyes met, his hand hovering, aware of her soft skin beneath the fingers of his other hand. He felt an imprudent urge to lean a little closer, to…

He dropped his hand, lowered his eyes and the moment was shattered.

She finished her mouthful and then laid the tortilla down, wiping her mouth herself just for good measure.

"That really put paid to my debut, didn't it?" she said with a light laugh. "Thanks."

Her joking manner eased them back into a more comfortable place.

"That's okay. Glad to help." Will lowered his own napkin to the table, surprised at how shaken he felt at that brief encounter.

"Should have ordered the pork roast, I guess. Of course that comes with gravy. Fries come with ketchup." She tilted her head, enumerating various other items on the menu and their disadvantages to her, then looked back up at him. "Can dress me up, but you can't take me out," she concluded with a smile.

Will was amazed at her self-deprecating wit, her ability to laugh at herself.

It was dangerously endearing.

"Do you go out much?" he asked, hoping his question didn't sound like he was fishing to see if she ever dated anyone else. Which he was.

Kelsey shook her head. "No. The restaurant and Chris take up a lot of time." She wiped her mouth again, her eyes flicking to his, then away.

It shouldn't matter to him if she went out every night of the week. He wasn't here to put the hustle on her. Ease some of the guilt he felt at not trying harder to connect with her.

But it still made him feel good that she didn't date much.

She asked him about the job they were working on now, asking him a few questions about things Chris had spoken of.

Will obliged, cutting up his steak as he spoke, trying to find the right time to bring up the other reason for the evening.

But not yet, he thought as Kelsey asked him another question, her smile quick. He knew she was proud, independent. He was afraid of her reaction if he offered money. He didn't want to break the spell of the evening.

They talked about Stratton, about some of the people. Kelsey's gentle humor easily showed her love for the town and the people who lived there.

Again Will found himself jealous of the roots she had put down, the history she had here.

Finally, the meal drew to a close and Will still hadn't found the right time to talk to her.

Kelsey sat back in her chair, fiddling with her hair again as the waiter cleared away their plates. "You said you had business to discuss..." Kelsey said, raising her eyebrows as if in question.

Will held her gaze but knew what he wanted to discuss with her would break the mood. "I did. But I've decided it can wait."

She declined dessert and when the bill was laid on the table, she tried to take it.

Will caught it in time. "My treat. I already told you," he said firmly.

Kelsey looked as if she might protest, then to his surprise, she shrugged lightly and tossed him another quick smile.

"Thanks, then. I appreciate it."

She picked up her purse, a signal that the evening was drawing to a close.

He got the hint and stood to help her up, but she

was already standing, lightly brushing the front of her dress.

"Whew," she said with a light laugh. "No crumbs, no stains. I did it."

"You sound surprised?"

"Surprised? For me, that's a miracle."

Will couldn't help but laugh.

They walked toward the front of the restaurant where a family waited to be seated.

"Kelsey, hello," the mother said.

"Hello, Anita. Michael." Kelsey paused to give the woman a quick hug, then stood back, her hand still on Anita's arm. "How are you doing?"

The woman lifted a hand, waggling it in an uncertain gesture. "I'm okay for now. The doctor was pleased with the results of the last test. But he wants to do more. I just hope I won't need any more treatments."

Kelsey rubbed her hand up and down the woman's arm in comfort. "I'm still praying for you."

Will could just hear the soft pronouncement and saw the tired smile on the woman's face.

"I took Mr. Legs," the little girl said, holding up a stuffed rabbit.

Kelsey easily knelt down, admiring the ragged-looking toy, her hand now resting on the little girl's shoulder. "That is one lucky rabbit, Elise, to be able to come here to eat."

Once again Will couldn't keep his eyes off her,

watching how easily she connected with these people. Anybody, he amended.

Mr. Legs got another pat, Anita another smile and then Janelle bustled up. She favored Will with a coquettish glance, then seated the family.

Kelsey walked into the cloakroom, and pulled her coat off the hanger.

Will was right behind her and easily plucked it out of her hands. She resisted a moment, then stopped, turning to allow him to help her.

He adjusted it, his hands lingering. But she moved away and that was the end of that.

He held open the door for her, then stayed at her side as she walked toward her car, her shoes clicking on the pavement of the parking lot. They walked through a cone of light then out, the semidarkness creating a cool intimacy.

She got to the car and unlocked it, but just before she opened the door, she turned back to Will.

"Thanks for a lovely evening, Will. I enjoyed it."

He shifted his weight to one foot, feeling as awkward as a teenager, a most unusual feeling for someone who prided himself on always being in control.

"I'm glad," he said. "We'll have to do it again sometime."

The overhead light cast shadows on her face, burnished her copper hair, illuminated her smile. "Maybe," she said vaguely, her voice tugged away by the faint breeze.

That same breeze swept a lock of hair across her face. It got caught on her lips.

They both reached for it at the same time.

As their fingers touched, it was as if they meshed of their own accord.

Will didn't stop to think, to analyze. He raised her hand to his mouth, touched his cool lips to its soft warmth.

He heard her swift intake of breath at the same time as he felt her fingers curl around his cheek. At her gentle response he turned his face to her touch, circling her wrist with his fingers, holding her hand there.

She whispered his name and to his ears it sounded like a prayer.

He couldn't stop himself as he slid his hand down her arm, pulled her close with his other hand. She drifted against him without resistance.

Then his mouth was on hers, his arms held her close. It was like coming home, he thought, as his eyes drifted shut, as his lips touched her cheek, her forehead, her temple, each kiss opening another part of his heart.

Her one hand clutched his back, the other held the back of his head as he sighed against her hair.

They stood quiet in the warm sanctuary they had created.

He stroked her hair with his chin, unexpected contentment stealing over him. This felt so right. It felt so good.

Then, imperceptibly at first, he could feel her withdraw. He murmured his dissent, tried to stop her.

But her hands slipped to his chest, exerting a gentle pressure.

"Please," she whispered, that single word wounding him more than he thought possible.

Her head was lowered, her hair slipping forward to cover her face.

"I get the impression that this is where I'm supposed to say I'm sorry, but I'm not, Kelsey."

She raised her head, her hand coming up to brush her hair back from her face. Her eyes glittered in the light. She held his gaze a moment, then without saying another word, ducked into her car.

He watched as she started it, confusion and yearning battling within him.

Kelsey curled up in her bed, her arms wrapped around her knees. A quick glance at the clock confirmed her suspicions. She'd been lying wide-awake for two hours.

She rolled to her other side, punched the pillow and dropped her head on it.

Again and again she felt the touch of Will's mouth on hers, of the warmth of his body as he held her close. Again and again she had tried to dismiss the feelings he ignited in her as the need of a lonely woman.

Will was not for her. In a few months he would be gone. She was crazy to give this night too much importance. She had her parents to think of, a child to raise, a restaurant to keep going. People counted on her. She had no emotional room to spin fantasies about a man like Will Dempsey. She still hadn't worked through her anger with Carter, his deception. She didn't know if she was ready to trust any man again.

She sat up, snapped on the light and pulled her Bible off the end table in an effort the stop the flow of her thoughts. She'd already done her devotions. But if she was going to lie awake anyway, she may as well read some more. Maybe it would help put Will back into his rightful place. Acquaintance. Friend. Partner of Carter.

She let the Bible fall open and started reading.

Psalm 85. "'Love and faithfulness meet together; righteousness and peace kiss each other,'" she read aloud. The insurgent beat of her heart made her stop.

Righteousness and peace kissing each other. She touched her own mouth and felt a sharp pain as she easily recalled Will's lips kissing her.

She closed her eyes, wishing she could rid herself of the feeling. It was loneliness she had told herself. It was just a yearning to be cherished, to be held. What single woman wouldn't want that?

But even as the rational part of her mind worked this through, another part of her vividly recalled his touch, the intensity of his gaze. She remembered the yearning she saw in his eyes both tonight and Sunday.

Will was lonely and he was seeking.

An alluring thought crept to the edges of her mind. Could she fill that need?

Would she want to?

With a guilty start, she pulled herself away from her wandering thoughts. "Forgive me, Lord," she whispered as she found her place again.

Verse 11. "'Faithfulness springs forth from the earth,'" she read aloud in an effort to concentrate, "'and righteousness looks down from heaven. The Lord will indeed give what is good, and our land will yield its harvest.'" She let the words sink into her mind, mulling over them, letting them comfort her. "'The Lord will indeed give what is good,'" she read again, making the words her own.

Her mind unwillingly went to the restaurant. To the burdens of trying to run it while her father slowly lost interest. To the memories that attacked her whenever she was feeling down.

She thought of the things she had to do yet. She wondered if Will had ever had financial trouble.

She wondered why her thoughts, like the needle of a compass, kept returning to him.

Help me trust you, Lord. Help me to let go of the things of this earth, to use the opportunities that You send my way. She paused a moment, realizing what she was asking. Then, with a gentle sigh, continued. *Help me to keep You first in my life.* Her prayer continued as she slowly laid her burdens on the Lord, slowly gave thanks in her current circumstances.

When she was done, she turned the light off and pulled the blankets up over her shoulders. But as she lay there in the dark, she couldn't erase the memory of the way Will's eyes crinkled lightly at the corners when he smiled, the intensity of his gaze whenever he looked at her. At that moment she wondered what business he said he had to discuss with her. It hadn't come up.

She pulled her knees up to her chest as if for protection and once again, thought of Carter. It was like a sore she couldn't leave alone.

And what do I do about that, Lord? She prayed. *Show me how I must act, how I can deal with this. It hurts so much and it makes me scared to trust again.* She thought of Will and how she had enjoyed being with him once she had relaxed. She remembered his smile, his touch. Was it right to put all her fears on his shoulders? Or any man's?

"Forgive, even as I forgave you." The words returned, haunting. And she knew what she had to do. She had to purposely forgive Carter. She had to let go of her anger with him. He was gone. He could hurt her no more. God was her faithful lover and friend.

"I want to be rid of this, Lord," she whispered laying her head on her knees. "I don't want anger to determine my life. I don't want it to eat away at me. I don't want to think that my love for Carter was a waste." She panicked a moment, as Lorelei's words spun back into her mind, hurtful and cruel. She took a deep breath, closing her eyes. *I loved him. I forgive him. I don't want him to have this power over me yet.* And as she slowly laid her burden on the Lord, as she slowly, deliberately thought of the hurt Carter had inflicted on her, she laid it to rest in God's hands. Let his justice and mercy do what she couldn't.

Forgive her dead husband.

"So. How was the lovely Kelsey Swain?" Drew asked as he jumped into Will's truck and pulled out his lunchbox.

"She's fine." Hearing Drew call her by her married name reinforced what he discovered last night.

"Okay. I sense a note of resistance. What happened?"

"Nothing."

"And I suppose that's part of the problem." Drew tossed Will a sly look.

Will wanted to ignore him as he had managed to with many other dates when Drew started in on his fussy matchmaker role. But Drew knew Carter as well and for the first time ever, Will felt a need to share this problem with his friend.

"Spill," encouraged Drew, as if sensing Will's wavering.

Will drew his hands over his face as he sucked in a breath. "She's still stuck on Carter."

"Do you think she knows about Carter? The truth?"

Will shook his head as he lowered his hands.

Thankfully this time Drew didn't say anything more.

Will leaned on the steering wheel, watching without interest as packers rolled down the roadbed in front of him thinking about Kelsey and Carter.

When Carter was alive, his knowledge of his partner's activities burned like a brand in his mind and he'd felt he should tell Kelsey.

But when he went to their home, when he saw Kelsey holding her baby son close with a contented smile on her face, he knew he couldn't.

Drew finished off his lunch and snapped the box shut. "So what are you going to do?"

"What's to do?" He rubbed the back of his neck, rolling his head. "I took her out for supper as a thank-you and she still talks about Carter." He flipped his hand dismissing the topic.

"What if it's self-defense?"

"You're a worse romantic than she is."

"You make it sound like a sickness."

"It isn't. But it also doesn't mean anything. My mother kept telling me what a romantic guy my dad was. She was as blind as Kelsey. I'm not getting tangled in that situation again." Will pulled his hard hat off the seat and picked up his gloves knowing that he was talking with more bravado than he felt.

But as he looked across the seat at Drew, he could see sympathy in his friend's eyes. "Just because she's loyal to Carter doesn't mean she's like your mother," Drew said quietly.

"My mother should have left my father years ago. Would have saved herself a lot of pain and bruises." Will dropped his hard hat on his head and was about to go, when he turned back to Drew. "What do you think Kelsey's life would have been like if Carter hadn't died?"

"That matters to you, doesn't it?"

Will sighed. "Much as I hate to admit it, she matters to me."

"This is a new thing for you. A woman that you've dated that matters to you."

Will said nothing, his feelings so unsure. What did he intend to do about it? His time here was temporary. What was he going to do when it was time to leave? Kelsey wasn't the sort of woman you just walk away from. He found with each moment he spent with her his life of moving around became less and less appealing.

"You know, Will, life isn't like a blueprint," Drew continued. "It isn't all mapped out and neat and tidy. You know that yourself. Sometimes you just have to see where things take you. Why don't you forget about Carter? Forget about who and what he was, forget that you're going to be leaving in a couple of months and concentrate on Kelsey. Take her out again. Spend some time with her. Try things on for size. If it doesn't work, it doesn't work. No different than any of the other women you've taken out."

Will heard Drew's advice. It sounded solid. The only trouble was, he didn't want to treat Kelsey like any of the other women he'd taken out. He didn't want to treat her like an experiment.

Because he also knew the more time he spent with her, the deeper his feelings grew.

Chapter Ten

Kelsey lifted her face to the sun, letting its warmth wash over her. As she did so, she felt a moment's regret for the amount of time she spent indoors. When she and Carter were married, she used to take Chris for long walks along the river, enjoying the fresh air. These days it seemed as if she spent most of her day inside the restaurant or trying to stay on top of housework and laundry.

Today was no exception. She had stayed at work as long as possible and then a quick stop at her parents' to pick up Chris. She could have let him stay there while she picked up groceries, but she felt they spent so little time together, she decided to take him along.

"Look, Mom. The fair. Can we go?"

Kelsey glanced up at the poster that had been stapled to the community bulletin board outside the grocery store. She had known about it and had harbored the idea of taking Chris to the fair. However the week had melted away and today was the last day.

"I don't know, dear." She thought of the limited amount of money she had in her wallet then looked down at her son who stared up at the brightly colored poster with a hungry look.

"Billy says they have a roller coaster and a Ferris wheel," Chris said wistfully. He glanced up at his mother, his nose wrinkled in question. "What's a Ferris wheel?"

Kelsey smiled wryly, tousling his hair. Chris had never been to a fair before, a thought that easily nudged guilt once more to the fore. "It's a big round wheel that has seats on it and it goes around."

"Can we go?"

"I don't know, sweetie. I'll think about it." And think about it was probably all she could do.

Chris gave the poster one more yearning look, then trudged into the store behind his mother.

Kelsey worked quickly through her list and by the time she pushed the cart to the lineup at the cashier, she was tired and Chris was cranky.

She dug in her purse and pulled out a coin. "Here," she said, handing him the money, "go get some gum." Bribery always worked and she wasn't averse to using it. Not after a day like today.

Chris brightened and working his way through the lineup, managed to get to the gum machine.

Kelsey leaned on her cart, her eyes wandering

with disinterest over the magazine racks as she slowly pushed her cart ahead. Women with perfect hair and perfect teeth smiled their perfect smiles back at her. She wondered if any of them ever had to buy groceries, mentally adding up the amounts in their heads. She wondered if any of them had to try to find money lost in a tangle of bad bookkeeping. She wondered if any of them had to forgive their husbands.

She supposed they did. What had happened to her was almost mundane these days. Whenever she read about it, or heard about it, it had begun to seem normal. Sad, but normal.

Until it happened to you, she thought sadly. Then it tore and broke and hurt. And it was almost worse when there was no one to yell at.

Maybe just as well.

Behind her, someone cleared his throat, yanking her back to the present. The person ahead of her was done and she was next in a growing lineup.

She hauled her groceries out of the cart, setting them on the already revolving turntable. By the time she was done, she realized Chris hadn't come back.

She felt a mother's momentary panic as she searched the store. Then she saw him, still at the gum machine.

He was talking to Will.

Kelsey's throat went dry, her heart quickened its tempo. All week he had been in her thoughts. All week she had casually walked through the restaurant at supper time, wondering if he might be there, relief vying with disappointment when he wasn't.

Now he stood beside her son, his very presence creating a sense of expectation.

Of course she would have to meet Will looking like this. No makeup, her hair twisted up and anchored with an unsightly plastic clip. Kelsey glanced down at the ketchup stain on her blue jeans from lunch, the line of dust on her T-shirt from digging through the old files.

She looked a sight.

Will, however, didn't. His dark hair had been tamed, emphasizing his faint widow's peak. His tan shirt was crisp and clean, as were his blue jeans. Even his cowboy boots were polished.

He stood, talking to Chris, his weight resting on one leg, his thumbs hooked in his belt loops, a smile crawling across his lips. As Kelsey watched, two women slowed as they passed him, giving him a second glance.

He didn't even notice.

"That will be $75.06, please," the cashier said.

Kelsey whipped her head around, momentarily flustered, thankful Will hadn't caught her looking.

"Pardon me?" she asked.

The cashier repeated the amount and Kelsey opened her purse. She pulled some bills out of her wallet and handed them to the cashier.

The girl glanced down at the money, then back at Kelsey. "That's not enough, ma'am."

Kelsey frowned, looking at the amount on the

cash register, then at the bills in the girl's hand. She was five dollars short. "Oh, I'm sorry," she said.

Pull it back together, Kelsey, she reprimanded herself. Will shows up and you fall apart. She opened her wallet, but it was empty. A flush warmed her cheeks as she glanced at the amount again. She set the wallet aside and rummaged through her purse hoping to find something, anything. All she managed to scrounge up was an assortment of quarters and nickels. Not enough.

Her cheeks grew even redder as she glanced at the bagged groceries on the cart.

"I'll have to put something back, I'm afraid," she said feeling more foolish as people behind her in the lineup began to shuffle and mutter. She was so sure she had added everything up correctly.

The cashier sighed her displeasure and pulled the cart back. "What do you want me to take out?"

That's when Kelsey felt him. Felt his height, his breadth. He hadn't touched her, hadn't even spoken, but she was as aware of Will Dempsey standing beside her as if he had.

"Here. That should cover it."

As Kelsey glanced sideways, she saw him hold out a five-dollar bill.

She was mortified.

"No. That's okay," she said quietly, hoping only Will and the cashier could hear her. "I'll just put some groceries back." She chanced a quick look up at Will.

He wasn't even looking at her.

"Please, Will. It's fine," she said again her embarrassment growing.

But the cashier had already finished the transaction and only when she handed Kelsey the bill, did Will give her a quick glance.

He looked implacable and for a moment Kelsey felt as if she had been the one that erred instead of him.

"I could have taken care of it," she said, banking her own animosity.

"Shall we go?" he said, placing a hand on her shoulder and exerting a gentle pressure. "People are waiting."

Kelsey glanced back at the customers behind her, some openly expressing their impatience.

She wanted to protest but realized how childish that would be. It was only five dollars. She could pay him back.

She relented. "Thank you very much," she said zipping up her purse and bestowing what she hoped was a mature-looking and properly grateful smile as they walked around the counter to their cart.

His hand lingered a moment on her shoulder, then he withdrew it. "You're most welcome," he said.

Kelsey wished he hadn't moved his hand. Wished he'd left it there a moment longer. For a moment she had felt cherished. Cared for. For a moment she needed that feeling badly.

"Mommy, Will got me a gum, too," Chris called out, bounding up to her, his mouth rimmed in red.

"I see that." She pulled a tissue out of her purse and kneeling down, wiped his mouth.

"Did you think about it, Mom?" he asked, his eyes wide with expectation.

"Think about what, honey?" Kelsey gave his mouth another wipe and straightened.

"The fair. Can we go?"

Kelsey thought of the transaction of a moment ago, wondered how she was going to tell him, in front of Will, that they couldn't afford to go. It would be too humiliating. "How about we just go and walk around the fairground. Have a look? Okay?"

"And can we ride on the Ferris wheel?"

Chris was relentless and Kelsey replied with the age-old answer parents use to weasel out of situations.

"We'll see."

Chris must have sensed that this was the only concession he was going to wring out of her for now because he didn't push anymore. He turned to Will. "Are you coming with us to the fair? Can he, Mom?"

"I think that's up to Will, don't you?" she said, putting her purse in the grocery cart.

"Can you come, Will? Please?"

After not seeing him for a week and then having him show up in time to pay for her groceries, Kelsey felt torn between a desire to have Will leave and to have him stay.

Yet, woven through those emotions was the memory of last week and his unexpected kiss. She didn't know what it meant, and for a while didn't care.

"Let's first get these groceries to your mom's car, okay?" Will said to Chris, his tactful comment giving them both a bit of space.

But it took no time to put the few bags in her car. Then they stood in the parking lot, an awkward silence hanging between them.

Chris didn't notice, he was busy bouncing on the car seat, playing with the window.

Kelsey finally dared look up at him again. "I know I said it already, but thanks for helping me out back there. I'll pay you back...."

"Don't start with that, Kelsey. It was only five bucks." He slipped his hands in the back pocket of his blue jeans.

"Well, it was embarrassing."

Will shrugged it away.

"So, did you get your own grocery shopping done?" Kelsey asked, hoping her tone conveyed a mere casual interest. She hadn't seen him all week and to her surprise had missed him.

Will looked down at her then, his eyes holding hers. "I didn't come here to buy groceries. I saw your car. That's why I came into the store."

Kelsey tried to hold his steady gaze, tried not to wonder at the implications of what he said.

"I was thinking of taking you and Chris to the fair."

Kelsey couldn't stop the smile that pulled on her mouth, the warmth that suffused her as he looked at her, his features softened by the smile that curved his mouth. She tried to stop herself, tried to remind herself of Carter. Tried to think of a hundred reasons she shouldn't go with this man.

But it was just a fair. And she had promised Chris. And if they didn't go, she would just sit at home, trying to wade through her father's horrible bookkeeping. That was hardly fair to her son.

And Will had asked them to come.

"Okay," she said, feeling slightly breathless. "Just let me bring my groceries home. I can meet you there." If she hurried, she could effect a quick change of clothing—try to repair some of the damage the day had inflicted. Try to look less like a mommy and more like a woman.

"I'll follow you," he said, raising one eyebrow. "But this time I'm driving you to the fair."

Kelsey returned his smile. "Okay. See you at my house, then."

Will pulled up in front of Kelsey's house, smiling at the row of blue pansies edging her sidewalk. The very first time he had come here, she'd had yellow pansies. The next year, purple.

The beds against the house and the pots hanging from the porch all spilled out flowers in a profusion of colors and types.

It looked like a home.

He got out of the truck and strode up the walk. As he got closer he noticed one of the boxes had fallen down and was lying in the flower bed, dirt spilling out on the plants.

He paused a moment, noticing where it had hung before.

The screen door slapped open and Chris called out to him. "My mom is just about ready. She's pulling faces in the mirror."

Will laughed at that. "What do you mean?"

"You know." Chris pulled his mouth open, held his eyes wide as he pretended to put on mascara.

Will felt a light upward lift at the thought of Kelsey getting ready. For him.

He looked away from Chris, who was hanging over the railing. "Do you know if your mom has a screwdriver?"

"My daddy had tools in the garage."

"Why don't you show me?"

Conveniently, Will also found a few screws and in a matter of minutes, he had the box back up and the dirt cleaned up from the flower bed.

"You fix things good," Chris said admiringly.

"I should wash my hands," Will said, brushing the dirt off as best he could.

He turned to see Kelsey standing on the porch looking down on him, her expression oblique. For a moment he wondered if he had overstepped his bounds.

"Thank you seems to be the word of the day," she said, folding her arms over her chest. She had changed into other clothes, he noted. At the grocery store she looked cute with her hair all mussed and her cheeks flushed. Natural.

But this Kelsey looked mighty fine, too, he thought, taking in her cream sweater and khaki pants and the mascara that emphasized her green eyes.

"I've been meaning to put that up but just never had the time," she continued.

"Well, you're welcome. I'll add it to the bill."

She smiled at that, and Will felt exonerated.

"I'd like to wash my hands and then I guess we can go," he said.

She stood aside and as he passed her caught a faint whiff of her perfume. Light and flowery like her.

As he stepped inside the house, the feeling of familiarity that permeated this home overcame him.

It was just that he'd been here before, he rationalized. But when Chris followed him into the bathroom, chattering as Will washed his hands, telling him about his day at his grandparents', it was as if something missing in his life drifted just within his grasp.

And when he looked up to see Kelsey in the doorway, watching him, the missing part fell into place. This was a home. A place where people were welcome. A place a person could return to feeling as if all that was important was held by these four walls.

A place where love overflowed.

He turned away, wiping his hands, the realization rocking him to the core. He tried to fight it, tried to rationalize his way around it, but when he looked at her again, he sensed a connection, a belonging that he had never felt with any other woman before.

Kelsey held Chris's hand as they started walking toward the fairgrounds. The smell of hot dogs and popcorn mingled with that indefinable aroma peculiar to fairs.

The tinny music of the carousel came in snatches between louder rock and roll that accompanied some of the other rides. All of it was laced with the sounds of children squealing their delight and barkers shouting advertisements of their games.

For a moment she wondered at the wisdom of coming here. While Will was putting up the window box, she had been frantically scrounging through the house, and luckily found some spare change. Enough for one ride on the Ferris wheel. How was she going to explain to Chris, in front of Will, that he would only be able to go on one ride? She knew what would happen. Will would offer to pay, and she would feel embarrassed all over again.

It would have been easier to stay home.

But that would have meant missing out on being with Will who now strolled easily alongside them, holding Chris's other hand.

Kelsey couldn't stop another quick sidelong glance at Will. His eyebrows weren't angled down in his perpetual frown of concentration. His mouth was softened by a smile. He looked more relaxed than she'd seen him in a while and her heart quickened in response.

As if he'd heard it, he angled his head, his eyes catching hers. Then he smiled and Kelsey's heart missed its next beat.

"So, Mr. Dempsey, how many times have you been to a fair?" she said quickly, covering up her reaction to him.

He shook his head, his smile broadening. "Believe it or not, this is my first time."

"Are you kidding?" she asked, incredulous. "How in the world could you have never gone to a fair?"

He shrugged. Looked away. "By being on the road every single summer, I guess."

Little comments he had dropped at their dinner together melded. She knew he wouldn't appreciate it, but Kelsey felt a moment's sympathy for him.

"Too bad this couldn't have been a more fullblown affair," she said with a light laugh. "Stratton just gets the small stuff."

"Looks good enough for me," he said.

They strolled down the small midway, stopping to watch people play games.

"Can I try, Mom?" Chris asked right on schedule.

Avoiding Will's gaze Kelsey said firmly, "No, honey. We're just walking around for now."

"Just one?" he reiterated.

Kelsey tightened her grip on his hand and tugged lightly, hoping her actions would speak louder than words. Her accompanying frown must have done the trick because Chris stopped.

The singsongy whine of the carousel started up, and they stopped to watch. Chris squeezed Kelsey's hand even tighter, his head bobbing as he watched the brightly decorated horses jerking past him.

They wandered a little more. Chris was uncharacteristically silent and Kelsey's discomfort grew with each quiet moment.

"I'm going to try this game," Will said suddenly, stopping in front of a booth. After paying the attendant, he was handed five balls. He frowned at them, then at the targets.

"Chris," he said quietly, giving Kelsey a quick glance. "Maybe you could show me how to do this."

Chris's eyes lit up and he bounded over, only too pleased to be showing the man he adored how to do something. "It's so easy, Will. You just have hit the squirrels with the balls."

Kelsey didn't know where Chris got his sudden knowledge. That child had never played an arcade game in his life.

"I don't know. I still don't get it. Why don't you show me?"

Chris gladly obliged, crowing when one of the squirrels fell over with the second ball. The third one flew wide.

"Good trick," murmured Kelsey as Will stood back beside her. She glanced sidelong at him, unable to stop her smile.

Will shrugged, his brown eyes drifting down to

hold hers. "I had to find a way around his very proud mother."

She held his gaze as memories of their last time together shivered through her mind. Her eyes moved downward to his lips, soft, inviting.

Then to her shock and surprise, she felt his hand rest on her shoulder, felt his fingers brush her neck.

She didn't move. Couldn't. Instead she felt an intense urge to lean toward him, to touch him.

"I got another one down, Mommy," Chris cried out.

Kelsey tore her gaze away from Will's, blushing as she confronted her excited son.

"Good for you, Chris." She injected a false enthusiasm into the automatic words as she gathered her dazed senses.

Will lowered his hand.

She stepped away.

But as they walked together down the midway she was aware of every move he made.

Will "tried" a few more games, Chris only too happy to "teach" him. Kelsey watched, unable to banish the feeling of absolute rightness in Will's easy manner with Chris.

She couldn't keep her eyes off him as Will patiently listened to Chris's exuberant explanations. Couldn't stop watching him as he straightened.

When Chris went on the merry-go-round, Will stood beside her, waving to Chris as he came by. He didn't touch her again, but he didn't have to. His nearness was as compelling as a touch, his presence behind and beside her like a sanctuary.

She couldn't stop the dangerous game she played, allowing herself to weave even the faintest fantasy around this man. Her loneliness was a quiet echo when she was with him.

As the sun set, the lights of the midway became brighter and the noise level higher. Kelsey shivered in the gathering coolness, wishing she had taken a sweater.

"Do you want to go?" Will asked.

She shook her head, unwilling to return to the reality of single parenthood and the emptiness of her home. This was time out of time, a memory she could take out once Will was gone.

"Can I go on the Ferris wheel now, Mom?" Chris asked, bouncing beside her.

Kelsey glanced at her watch

"Why don't we all go?" Will said quietly.

Kelsey glanced his way, then nodded her acquiescence. "That sounds like fun."

So they made their way to the Ferris wheel, waited their turn in line.

"Hi, Chris." A young boy ran up to her son. "You going on the Ferris wheel? I'm going with my dad."

Chris looked at his friend Randy, then back at Will and Kelsey.

She could see the confusion in his eyes and wondered again at the wisdom of spending time with Will. What would Chris think when Will was gone?

But she didn't have a chance as Randy and his father got in their seats. Next up was Will, Kelsey and Chris. Chris wanted to sit on the outside, and Kelsey got the middle.

As the chair rose up in the gathering dusk, Will settled back, slipping his arm around her shoulders. She shivered again, his arm tightened and Kelsey's doubts fled.

Then the Ferris wheel rose up into the night, swinging. Kelsey clung to the bar in front.

"You scared?" Will asked, his fingers brushing her shoulder.

"Of course not," she said, glancing back at him, wishing she could find the bantering tone she so easily used with other men. But it eluded her as she caught his gaze.

Other emotions swirled beneath the surface of her relationship with this man. Emotions that threatened to pull her into a place where she had no defenses against him. No assurances.

And yet she couldn't look away, couldn't stop as he slowly drew her against him, his arm warm and hard across her shoulders.

"Look, Mommy. I think I can see our house." Chris was leaning away from them, oblivious to the tableaux playing out behind him. "And my school."

He continued his monologue as Kelsey sat tucked up against Will. She closed her eyes and sent up a prayer.

Help me, Lord. I'm scared and confused. I don't

*know what he wants and I'm too afraid to confront
him. I enjoy his company too much.*

But even as she prayed, she let her head rest
against Will's shoulder, sighed as she felt his lips
touch the top of her head.

Time out of time, she reminded herself, moving
her cheek lightly against the rough material of his
shirt.

She rested her hand on his knee and let time roll
along as slowly as the wheel they were suspended
in.

All too soon the ride came to an end. Without
looking at Will, Kelsey got out of the chair. Taking
Chris by the hand, they walked down the midway
toward the truck.

As they got in, with Chris between them, Kelsey
couldn't even look at Will, afraid of what would
happen if she did.

Chris yawned as Will pulled out of the parking
lot, laid his head on Kelsey's lap and promptly fell
asleep.

When they got to Kelsey's home, Will silently
picked Chris up and carried him into the house, Kelsey following behind him.

Will laid Chris on the bed and Kelsey took over,
pulling off his shoes and socks, putting his pajamas
on.

All this was done in silence, a sense of waiting
hovering over the two of them.

Kelsey closed the door of the bedroom and
walked to the living room, Will right behind her.

Her steps slowed as she approached the couch. Above the wall behind it, hung a picture of Carter.

And in the glass she saw a reflection of Will.

She shivered, wondering what, if anything, it meant. Wondered what, if anything, would come out of this evening. She was going farther and farther down a road that had no directions, no signs. Will may have kissed her, may have put his arm around her, but nothing else had changed.

She didn't expect immediate declarations of love, yet as a single mother, she knew she wasn't being fair to her son by spending time with this man.

But she couldn't face the idea of not being with him. And that was what frightened her.

Chapter Eleven

$\smile$

Will stood behind Kelsey, her arms folded across her stomach as she faced straight ahead.

Looking at a picture of Carter, he thought with dismay.

"I want to thank you for a lovely time," she said quietly, her back still to him. "Chris had fun and I really enjoyed myself."

Turn around, he thought. Let me see your face. Let me see that you mean what you say.

Half an hour ago, she had sat tucked against him and for a few moments he felt as if he had found the emotional center of his life.

Now that she was home, back in the house she and Carter had shared, he could feel her retreating.

"I had a good time, too," he said.

Kelsey turned then, smiling, and Will relaxed slightly. "Do you want a cup of coffee?" she asked.

Surprise sluiced through him at the unexpected invitation. "Sure. That would be nice."

And once again he settled himself on a couch in her living room as she busied herself in the kitchen.

A few moments later she handed him a mug then dropped into the chair across from him, holding her mug close.

Will took a sip of coffee, unsure of how to proceed. They had spent time alone before, had gotten to know each other better. It was as if they were now sidestepping a place each was reluctant to enter.

His eyes fell on a row of cards Kelsey had placed on the mantel. Birthday cards. He frowned.

"Was it your birthday?"

Kelsey shook her head, looking away. "No. I was cleaning up some boxes the other day. Those were cards Carter used to send me. Chris wanted to put them up."

Carter again.

"He often sent you cards, didn't he?"

Kelsey nodded, her finger tracing the top of her mug.

"Flowers, too?"

"You should know." Kelsey looked up at him, holding his gaze, a question flickering in the depths of her eyes.

"Is that important to you?" he asked, unsure of what she seemed to want from him.

Kelsey shrugged, glanced at him, then away. "At one time it was, I guess."

Will felt as if each word pierced him.

"Didn't you ever send the women you were dating flowers?" Kelsey asked.

Will shook his head. "No, never did."

"Why not?"

"Is this a test?" he asked, feeling defensive.

"No. Just curious." Kelsey held his gaze, her own soft, compelling. "Actually, I'm more than curious. I guess I'm interested in what makes you tick. Who the real Will Dempsey is."

"He's a very boring person."

"When I saw you in church, I was intrigued. I thought you looked a little lost. Confused."

Will sighed, leaning back on the couch, remembering the feelings that had surrounded him, pulling him along. The control he tried to maintain. "It was an emotional experience. I guess that's the only way to describe it."

"And you're not comfortable with emotions."

Will frowned. "That's a bit harsh."

"But true?" Kelsey held his gaze, her own steady.

Will took a gulp of coffee. Even Drew wasn't this incisive with his questions.

"I've seen the result of emotions out of control. At home. My father had a wicked temper."

"You alluded to that the other night. What was he like?"

Will swirled his coffee around his cup, debating what to say. He'd never opened up to any woman he'd been dating. Just made things easier. He didn't know if he could change that habit. Didn't know how Kelsey would react to what he had to say.

He glanced at the cards on the mantel again, wondering if she would understand. She to whom those cards and flowers meant so much.

"Please tell me," she said quietly.

Will drew his hand over his mouth as he looked at her, then decided, not yet. He hardly dared look at Kelsey, knowing he was veering too close to a place he had to avoid.

She put her cup down and came to sit beside him. "You look so serious. I'm sorry if I'm being intrusive."

He looked at her then and couldn't stop his hand from coming up, from stroking her hair away from her face, from cupping her cheek.

She drifted toward him.

He lowered his head, his arms catching her close, his mouth touching hers. Her lips were soft, warm, inviting.

Her hand curled around his neck, holding his head and Will felt a melting in the deep recesses of his heart. He felt as if he had come to a place of refuge.

She broke away, but lay her head against his shoulder. Will's eyes drifted shut as he inhaled the gentle scent of her perfume mingled with the clean smell of her hair. He tangled his fingers in her hair, stroking the back of her head, her head tucked under his.

It was so right.

Can this be? The questions drifted up through his

consciousness. Can this possibly be? This woman, this life? Her faith is so strong, can I share it? Can I do it?

He tried to dampen the doubts, tried to erase them. She was as fooled by Carter as my mother was by my father, he thought.

Should that matter?

He rubbed his cheek over her hair as he fought to maintain the peace he had tasted. He drew in a deep breath, his arms tightening around her as he struggled to hold the doubts at bay.

As if sensing his misgivings, Kelsey drew back, a light frown wrinkling her brow. She reached up and ran her fingers lightly over his cheeks, traced the line of his eyebrows.

"Is something the matter?" Her soft question reinforced his feelings.

He dropped a quick kiss on her forehead, touched his lips to her cheek as if taking what he could right now.

Then as he pulled back, he looked away from the question in her eyes, wondering at the emotions that had beguiled him.

She had come willingly to his arms, had returned his embrace. All done with a gentleness that was her hallmark. It created a confusion that was both welcome and yet encroaching.

He had never been in this predicament before, had never felt the least bit vulnerable or doubtful with a woman. But Kelsey had him all twisted around.

He hated it.

He needed it.

Will touched her face, as if memorizing it. In spite of his misgivings, his inability to articulate his feelings for her, he wanted to spend time with her, even if only for a while. He was tired of being alone, lonely.

"Can I pick you up for church Sunday?" he asked suddenly, before the faint impulse was worn away by his ever present common sense. "I have to leave right after for Drayton Valley, but I would like to spend the morning with you."

"Of course." She smiled at him. "After all, any friend of Carter is a friend of mine."

She was making a joke, giving him some of the space he needed. Will knew that.

But as he looked past her at the picture of Carter on the wall and the line of cards on the mantel, he wondered if he was making a big mistake.

He turned back to her, and dropped a quick kiss on her forehead as if to erase the thought.

Will sat on the edge of the soft chair, his elbows resting on his knees, his hands loosely clasped. He resisted the urge to tap his thumbs together.

His own thoughts veered between anticipation and second thoughts. Taking Kelsey to church wasn't the same as taking Kelsey to the fair. Church wasn't a social thing. He knew that. But he was sitting in her living room now and it wasn't really the time to change his mind. Besides, he reminded himself. It was just a church service. He had to leave once it was over. He had an out.

Kelsey was in Chris's bedroom with her mother, doing the worried mother thing.

Chris had woken this morning with a fever and a sore throat. By the time he had arrived, Kelsey's mother was already here.

Thankfully Kelsey still wanted to come with him, but was feeling guilty about leaving Chris.

He smiled, thinking of how she alternately hovered over Chris and yet was able to give him independence. In spite of her own misgivings, she was a caring and loving mother.

"Thanks for coming here, Mom," Kelsey said as she walked into the living room ahead of her mother. "I really appreciate it."

"Chris will be fine. I'm sure he's just a bit overtired." Donita Hartley favored Will with a quick glance, her expression guarded. "Hello, Mr. Dempsey."

Will didn't imagine the cool note in her voice.

Kelsey hadn't, either, if her frown was any indication.

She looked as if she was about to say something, but Will forestalled her.

"We should go, Kelsey." Whatever Mrs. Hartley's reasons were for her reserved attitude, he didn't want to create any discord between daughter and mother.

Kelsey favored her mother with another glance,

then gave her a quick hug. "Thanks again, Mom. I'll see you after church."

"Take care, Mrs. Hartley," he said as they were leaving.

"You, too, Mr. Dempsey."

Will took a deep breath as he closed the door behind him. Definitely cool.

He put the scene behind him as he followed Kelsey down the walk. She wore pants today in a navy-blue with a matching thigh-length blazer. The color would have looked reserved and understated on most women but Kelsey's bright hair set it off, made it sparkle.

As he opened the door for her to get in, she grinned up at him.

"Did I tell you how good you look in a suit?" An impish smile curled her mouth.

Bemused, he shook his head. "No. Haven't heard."

"It makes you look suave, civilized."

"As opposed to..."

Kelsey tilted her head to one side, as if considering. "The rugged workingman look," she said.

As she grinned up at him, Will had to resist the urge to touch her hair, to drop a kiss on her smiling mouth, she looked so adorable.

He wondered how he was going to get through the church service, he thought, as he pushed her door shut.

They were at church early, and the usher seated them near the back, which suited Will just fine.

They settled into the pew, and Kelsey read the bulletin handed out by the usher. Will leaned back, his arms crossed as he studied the congregation filing in.

Families and elderly people mingled with teenagers and single men and women. A real cross section of humanity.

Every now and then Kelsey would look up, smiling in response to a greeting from fellow congregants. Will got a puzzled glance from some, a smile from others and a wink from Cory.

"Do you want to read the bulletin?" Kelsey asked, handing him the paper.

He looked at it then back at her. "Sure," he said, taking it from her. Most of it was a listing of various events taking place during the week. Meetings and classes and all those fussy, busy things that churches seemed to fill their time with.

He wondered what it would be like to sit in this church every Sunday, looking at the week ahead and reading reminders of other obligations. He glanced sidelong at Kelsey again who was having a whispered conversation with an elderly woman. The woman patted her on the shoulder then walked away, smiling. He wondered what it would be like to be a part of this community with Kelsey at his side.

Kelsey flowed through this community dispensing her charm, her smiles, her light touches that so easily created a connection. It was that same touch that she had so lightly bestowed on him the first time he had come to her restaurant, all those years ago.

His mind went easily back to that time.

He'd been on the road, checking things out when he'd stopped at her father's restaurant. She'd taken his order, chatted a moment and when she brought it to him, she'd laid her hand lightly on his shoulder and told him to enjoy his meal.

Her casual touch conveyed a sense of caring that went deeper than the male-female stuff he'd indulged in. But when Carter had accompanied him on another visit, Carter had dominated the conversation. And had won Kelsey over.

The burst of sound from the musical group at the front of the church pulled him back to the present. Just as before, the congregation got to their feet and started singing.

Kelsey was clapping, smiling, her eyes bright, her hair flowing as she sang along. Will couldn't keep his eyes off her. As if she sensed his regard, her eyes flitted up to him. Again the connection, the awareness arced between them.

Will rested his hands on the pew in front of him, clutching it to keep from touching her. In church of all places. He should be ashamed.

Yet he couldn't conjure up the emotion. It felt pure and right.

He concentrated on the song instead and on the other reason he'd asked to accompany her to church. He could have taken her out tomorrow or any other time this week, but he felt a hunger, a need to be here, in church, with her beside him.

Support? Encouragement? A reminder for him that to Kelsey, God was real and that he could have that for himself if only he took the time?

Will didn't sing along, but once again read the words on the overhead, concentrating. They were just words. It was just a song.

And yet it was more.

The song was a cry, a response to God's calling in the night.

Will knew well about those dark, lonely hours. Two in the morning, when sleep eluded him and it was as if all the mistakes he had made, all the missed chances were piled on his lonely soul. He had always felt something, someone drawing on him. His grandmother would have said it was God, but Will had dismissed God from his life as he grew older.

Now, as he stood in a church, reading the words to this haunting song, he knew with a quiet, definite knowledge, that God had been steadily seeking him. Seeking to draw Will into Him. He closed his eyes, resistance his first reaction. But he knew with a definite knowledge, he would have to face this again. And again.

Just as his grandmother had said the last time he had visited her.

Then, as the chorus began, "Here I am Lord..." his heart melted and all the barriers he had so painstakingly erected against God and emotions and feelings, toppled as easily as a child's block house.

He swallowed the knot of emotion and lowered his head.

Forgive me, Lord, he prayed, clutching the bench in front of him even harder. *Forgive this hardened heart. Forgive my lack of caring.*

He felt a wave of love so pure and so full it made his heart ache with wonder.

Thankfully the song was over, because he couldn't stand up, he was so overwhelmed by it.

As he sat down, he opened his eyes and drew in a deep breath, still feeling shaken by his encounter.

"Are you okay?" Kelsey laid her hand on his arm.

Will looked down into eyes tinged with concern. He covered her hand with his and smiled back at her.

"I'm fine," he replied. Then, without stopping to think or plan or wonder at repercussions, he pulled her hand through his arm and wound his fingers through hers.

Kelsey squeezed Will's hand as they stood up for the final benediction. He hadn't let go of her hand all service. She didn't want to examine the implications of that. She just knew that while they sang the last song of the gathering songs, something had touched him. She could feel it. And when he had taken her hand in his, it was as if they established a connection beyond touch.

As if God's love flowed powerfully through them both.

She bent her head, their fingers still entwined as she prayed. Her mind was a jumble of thank you and questions, and even in spite of what had just happened, she knew that with Will, whatever was happening between them, had to be handled moment by moment.

The notes of the last song faded away. The organist paused a moment and then started the postlude.

Kelsey couldn't help but look up at Will. His dark eyes met hers, soft and warm and Kelsey felt a shiver trickle down her back.

"I'm glad you came, Will," she said quietly, knowing that as soon as she turned around, she would be drawn into other people's lives.

"I'm glad I came, too," he returned, his expression pensive. He drew in a deep breath as he shook his head. "I don't know how to explain...."

"You don't have to. Not now," she said, her other hand rubbing his forearm. "We can talk later."

He gave her hand one final squeeze and then slowly released her.

She wanted to say more but someone touched her shoulder and reluctantly she turned to see who it was and what he or she wanted.

It was just Mrs. Bodean, who had noticed Kelsey's father sitting alone in church and diplomatically asked why.

As Kelsey chatted with her, she could feel Will behind her. Solid, strong and just for a moment she indulged in a fleeting fantasy. Together, her and Will, united as husband and wife.

She caught herself. Will had given her absolutely no indication of anything beyond casual dating. What they had shared moments before was spiritual.

She sighed as she went through this hovering between emotions and reality.

Outside the sun shone in bright intensity, as if reinforcing the day's name. Sunday. Day of rest.

Kelsey turned to Will just as they stepped out of the doors, determined not to get pulled into another conversation with someone else. The walk to his truck, however, was silent. As was the ride home. She wanted to know what Will was thinking, but his composed features gave her pause.

He stopped in front of her home then went around to her side of the truck to let her out. They walked up to the house, again in silence.

He stopped in front of her door, looking down at her. Still serious.

"Do you want to come in for lunch?" she asked, wanting to break the silence, to create the connection they had before.

Will had his hands in the pockets of his suit pants, his jacket open. An errant breeze lifted his tie, mussed his hair, softened the crisp lines the suit had created.

He looked down at her now, serious again.

"I'm sorry," he said quietly, "But I've got to go down to Drayton Valley right away."

Kelsey smiled through the last part of the sentence, portraying understanding and acceptance, even as the first two words he spoke struck against her heart like flint.

"Of course. I forgot," she said, determined not to let her foolish little fantasies interfere with the reality of Will's work. So had Carter often left her alone on Sundays. There was always a job that needed tending, workers that needed to be supervised. Always a job that took him away from home.

She knew this about Will. So the fact that disappointment rushed through her was her own fault. Not his.

"Well, I hope that you have a safe trip," she said, forcing a false cheeriness into her voice. She wasn't going to cling, she wasn't going to ask when he was coming back. She was determined to portray independence.

He frowned, as if this was not what he expected from her. They stood facing each other, uncertainty diverging with reality.

"I better go." Will hesitated a moment yet, then bestowed a faint smile on her and left.

Kelsey watched him stride away toward his truck, his tie fluttering in the wind. He didn't look back.

Will pulled off his tie and threw it on the couch, shrugged off his jacket and it went to the same place. He strode to the back of his trailer and quickly exchanged his suit pants and crisp white shirt for blue jeans and a work shirt.

He paused a moment, catching a glimpse of his reflection in the mirror.

He drew his hand over his face and blew out his breath. It was as if his neatly ordered life had just been tossed end over end and he was left clutching madly at the least thread. His so-called casual date with Kelsey hadn't assuaged the loneliness one ounce. All that it had done was create a sharper contrast between what he had and what he wanted.

Let go, let go, a voice urged him.

He didn't know if he dared. This morning in church, when the waves of emotion had roiled over him he had initially felt frightened, yet a peculiar peace had followed the chaos of feelings.

"What must I do?" he said aloud, dropping on the bed. He glanced at the minuscule end table built into the wall, beside his bed.

The Bible his grandmother had given him years ago lay there. He remembered Jean Payne reading the Psalms the best, so since his last visit to church, he had started there.

He picked it up again, leafing through it, as if searching for answers.

He knew his feelings for Kelsey grew, changed each time he saw her, each moment he spent in her presence.

Thinking of her brought up once again that confusion of emotions. He knew he cared for her. Had from the first moment she saw him.

But he also knew what she would require of him were he to allow himself to fall in love with her.

Commitment. Permanence.

A knock on his trailer door made him jump.

"Come in," he called out.

"I'm coming," Drew said, opening the door.

Will picked up his overnight bag, packed this morning and walked out of the bedroom. Drew was already sitting in an empty easy chair opposite the drafting table that took up most of the living space.

"What new calamity do you have to dump on me right now?" Will asked dropping his bag on the floor beside the drafting table.

"Nothing. Good news, actually. I just spoke to the engineer. He's going to authorize a partial payment for the job."

"That is good news."

"I thought that might put a smile on your face, but I see I wasn't successful."

Will ignored him. He picked up his cell phone and slipped it into the leather case.

"I heard you were in town last night," Drew continued, settling in for a heart-to-heart.

"You have excellent hearing," Will said dryly, dropping the phone into his overnight bag. "Did you hear I was in town this morning as well?"

Drew grinned. "Yeah. Church again. I think this Kelsey is a good influence on you."

Will refrained from commenting on that.

"So, what are your plans concerning her?"

"You never quit, do you?" Will asked, zipping up the bag.

"Why should I? I've never seen you this involved with a woman before."

"Hardly involved. We've only gone out a couple of times."

"And you've had her kid here...."

"Did you have anything more to say about work or anything else of importance before I leave?"

"You're sounding defensive." Drew leaned back and linked his hands behind his head. "I think you're falling for this woman."

Will felt a jolt at Drew's words, but wisely said nothing.

"Is the infamous Carter Swain still a stumbling block for you?" Drew looked up at Will, his expression suddenly serious.

Will thought of the cards Kelsey had lined up on her mantel. She had said Chris had put them there, but he wondered. "She has good memories of him."

"Aren't you worried that someone from this crew might tell her the truth sometime?"

"Not everyone knows."

"I think she should know."

Will took a deep breath as Drew relentlessly came back to the same thing. "And what purpose would that serve?"

Drew said nothing.

"He died in my arms crying out the name of a woman that wasn't his wife, Drew," Will said through clenched teeth. "Do you think I'm going to tell her that?"

Drew considered his friend, his gaze unyielding. "You've already told her part of the truth."

"And I've managed to destroy the memory she had of her husband."

"Carter wasn't a saint, Will. We all knew that. Now she knows part of it, too. Someday she might know more."

"Well, that might never come."

"C'mon Will. I see what's happening here. Did you think that you could get involved with her, that you could spend time with her and then just walk away? What about her son? How is he going to remember you?"

Will felt a pang of sorrow at what Drew said. Chris was a such a spunky kid. Each day he spent with him he appreciated him more and more.

"Of course it could be very convenient for you, couldn't it, this devotion to a dead husband."

"What do you mean?"

"It's easy for you." Drew stood up. "You can't measure up to this so-called saint. She can keep her memories and you can keep holding on to this heart that you hang on to so judiciously. It's convenient."

Will swung around, impaling his friend with his gaze. "And why would I need that?"

"Because you're a temporary guy, Will. Because

you're scared to settle down, to maybe think that somehow, somewhere you can create what you never had with your parents. A home. A family.''

Will picked up his bag and grabbed his coat from the hanger. He paused, then turned to his friend. "And what kind of example have I ever had of that in my life, Drew? A father who would just as soon hit me as hold me on his lap? A mother who ignored me because all her energy was poured into trying to please a man who couldn't be pleased?''

Drew looked at him, sympathy etched on his features. "You're a good man, Will. You don't give yourself enough credit. You would be a good father, a wonderful husband. You know how to do it because you know what you don't want a family to be like. And I know you would put your all into it.''

Will heard Drew, each word creating a new fear in him. Could he do it? Could it happen?

"I'll call you from Drayton," he said abruptly, pushing away his errant thoughts. Then he left.

But as he drove, Drew's words kept echoing in his ears. Questions slipped through his mind as quickly as the power poles beside him. He felt as if he were coming to a point that he had to decide, to choose.

He knew he couldn't be the man Carter was, at least in Kelsey's eyes. He didn't want to be. He wanted to be Will. His own person. Would what he knew about Carter cause a problem? Why did he even need to tell her? He didn't want to destroy her dreams. As he had told Drew, it would serve no purpose.

Yet, could he respect a woman who, like his mother, had been so blind to the reality of her husband?

And what about her faith? What did he know about serving God? About attending church regularly?

What did he know about raising a small child? What example had he had?

Help me through this, Lord. The prayer floated through his consciousness, unbidden.

Help? He had never needed help.

When Will had challenged his father and Sam Dempsey turned on him, was God there? Will had to face the enraged man on his own. He'd had to make his decisions on his own.

Help me, Lord.

Will swallowed as the same emotions he had felt this morning curled back, insidious in their gentleness.

Release, let go. Let God take control of life and emotions.

Help me, Lord.

Will drove on, wrestling, praying, confusion warring with the vulnerability of letting go. Ever since he had first stood up to his father, he had never allowed himself to be in any position where someone else had power over him.

Yet whatever he felt for Kelsey, for Chris, would require surrender.

The word frightened him and at the same time brought a measure of peace. Surrender meant he could stop fighting, stop trying so hard to be strong. Did he dare?

Chapter Twelve

Will stepped out of the truck and spun his keys around his finger as he looked over the parking lot of the restaurant. He noted with satisfaction that Kelsey's car was in its usual spot. She was here.

The guilt that had accompanied him from the job site in Drayton Valley melted like the last frost of spring. He felt as if he were coming to a place he wanted to be. A place he should be.

Never, in all the years of moving around had that ever happened. Never had he felt as if he didn't want to leave a place.

The idea made him smile. Not like my father after all, he thought. Overriding all the doubts he once had was a need that had been filled for the first time in his life. And in spite of his misgivings about her, Kelsey had done that.

The door to Kelsey's office opened and a woman

stepped out followed by an older man. They carried briefcases in one arm, trench coats over the other.

Bankers or lawyers or government people, Will guessed both by their unsmiling demeanor and their clothing. The man wore a suit, the woman a tailored dress.

Kelsey must have been expecting them, Will figured as he saw her pause in the doorway of her office. Her hair was pulled smoothly back from her face, and she wore the same suit she wore on Sunday. She meant business today, he thought.

She stood, arms clasped tightly across her stomach. Her face was set in determined lines, her usually smiling mouth looked grim.

"Thanks for coming," she said in a clipped voice. "I'll call you tomorrow and let you know my answer."

"That's fine, Kelsey. We can wait." The older man hesitated a moment, as if he wanted to shake her hand. But Kelsey was already retreating back into her office.

So he turned and walked past Will without giving him a second look. The woman followed right behind.

"Lousy bankers," a man behind him mumbled.

Will recognized Anton, one of the regulars. "How do you know?" he asked.

"Goodness, boy. Everyone in town knows the bankers. And Kelsey better than most." Anton snorted as he adjusted his stained baseball cap on the back of his head. "I'm guessing they're going to pull the plug on her. That poor woman's been working her fingers to the bone, trying to keep this place going,"

Anton rested his beefy hands on his hips, glancing at Will. "She don't deserve this, you know."

"I know," Will replied. He walked up to the door and knocked once, then quickly opened it.

"Come in," Kelsey said, leaning back in her chair, her stockinged feet on the wooden surface of the desk.

She raised her head and immediately her feet came down. Her wary look was replaced by a faint smile that drifted through him, catching him loosely by his heart.

"Hi, there," she said, getting up. She slipped her shoes on but stayed behind the desk. "What brings you to town?"

Will tried to think of an excuse, a reason, but couldn't. Dissembling wasn't one of his strong points.

"I thought I'd stop by. See how you're doing."

Will didn't think her smile could get any bigger. Didn't think he could react any stronger. He wanted to walk up to her and pull her into his arms, but a lifetime of reserve kept him in his place.

Again Kelsey came toward him. Again her light touch connected them, drawing him closer.

"I'm glad," she said, looking up at him.

Will closed the door behind him, to give them some measure of privacy. He lifted his hand and touched her cheek. Words clamored to be said, but his ever present caution kept them back. Wait, it said. Don't be too hasty.

"So, how have you been?" he asked, his eyes finding and holding hers.

She blinked, then looked away. "Okay. I've been okay."

"Anton told me the bankers were here."

Kelsey lowered her hands and pressed them together. "Anton talks too much," she said.

"What did they want, Kelsey?"

Kelsey sighed and turned away. "Just the usual banker-type stuff." She walked toward the window, her arms in that defensive posture again. "We had to go over our loan situation...."

Will could only guess what she meant by that, but his intuition and Anton's comments told him much more.

"What are your options?"

Kelsey raised one shoulder negligently. "Limited. Very limited."

"Selling isn't one of them."

"It's a possibility my father has been trying to avoid. I guess we can't now. I'll be phoning the real estate agent after this."

Turn around. Talk to me. Let me see what's in your eyes. Touch me again. But Kelsey kept staring out the window.

He remembered Chris's comment. Remembered seeing her at this very window. But how much could he assume? How much could he dare ask?

This was new territory for him. He had taken out

women before, but always managed to keep an emotional distance. Worked better that way. He had never been involved in their financial circumstances or their lives away from their relationship.

But Kelsey was different. Kelsey had always occupied a corner of his heart, had always been there. And now she had taken it over fully.

"So what happens if you don't sell this place?"

Kelsey rubbed her arms with her hands, still looking away from him. "I'm not sure."

He walked up behind her. Again he rested his hands on her shoulders, willing her to turn around.

"Kelsey, please tell me what's going on?"

She sighed and glanced back up at him. "I'm going to lose the restaurant. The bankers said unless a miracle occurs they're going to call in the loans."

"Which you don't have a hope of repaying." He let his hands linger, his fingers lightly caressing her shoulders.

She shook her head and looked away again.

Will slipped his hands down her arms and around her, pulling her against him. She leaned back, resting her head against his shoulder as he brushed a kiss across her temple.

All it took was a slight twist of her head as her breath brushed against his cheek and their mouths met in a gentle kiss. With a light sigh, Kelsey drew away, resting her head in the crook of his neck.

He didn't know what to say, afraid to articulate what was going through his mind. He knew that he had begun to care for this woman in ways he had never thought possible.

Tell her, tell her.

But he couldn't. Not yet.

Far better that he show her.

For now he was content to hold her, to comfort her, to feel as if he had finally come home.

And as he did, he knew what he had to do.

He drew away and Kelsey murmured her protest. She turned, resting her hands on his shoulders, her fingers brushing his neck. "So what really brings you to town today?"

Will looked down at her and tangled his fingers in her hair, just because he could. "I told you. You did," he said quietly, his eyes traveling over her face, as if memorizing her features.

She smiled, locking her hands behind his neck. "Well, that's an interesting incentive," she joked. "What in the world do I have to offer you?"

He heard the suppressed note of pain in her voice and his resolve became more sure. He dropped a kiss on her forehead and knew beyond a doubt, that what he wanted to do was the right thing. The best thing.

"More than you realize," he said softly, holding her suddenly close. He sighed lightly as they stayed thus, his heart overflowing.

Kelsey fiddled with some of the papers on her desk, filing some, rearranging others, her emotions a confusion of happiness and fear as she relived what happened yesterday again and again.

Did she dare trust another man? Did she dare trust Will? Even after yesterday, after being held by Will, Kelsey still wasn't sure what she meant to him. He said so little, held so much to himself.

Show me what to do, Lord, she prayed, dropping her head in her hands. *Help me deal with this. I'm alone and I'm scared. I think I'm falling in love with him. But I also know he's going to leave. Just like Carter always did.*

Kelsey knew that if she allowed herself to fall in love with Will, she would be devastated when he left.

The thought pulled her up short, sending ice through her veins. It was happening already.

Let go.

Let go of Will. Let go of the worry for her parents. Let go of so many things, she thought, looking down at the bundles of checks wrapped in bank statements.

Let go of the restaurant, she thought.

She didn't know how easy that was, either. If the restaurant didn't sell in the next few weeks, it would be taken over by the bank, Will would be gone…

The thought almost choked her. *Please, Lord, help me through this. I'm falling in love with him. He's becoming one of the reasons I wake up in the morning. Seeing him, even if it is only a glimpse makes all the difference to my day.*

And she had no concrete idea of how he felt.

Kelsey covered her face with her hands and bit her lip. Love was a risk. She knew that. She had risked much loving Carter and it had proved to be wrong. But she had forgiven that. Did she dare take the chance again? *Help me do this, Lord. Help me to let go of him, too. Help me to know that Your love is constant and true. Make me humble in faith and love.*

She drew in a slow breath and raised her head.

The first thing she saw were the bank statements from four years ago, the bound paper slowly uncurling. She had just found them this morning. At first she had been tempted to throw them away, but she needed to do something to keep her mind busy, so she pulled them toward her and started looking.

An hour later, Kelsey leaned back in her chair, frowning in puzzlement at what she had just discovered.

She had gone through the canceled checks that came with the statements. Each statement had one check missing, each for a substantial amount. Two checks for $25,000 and a final one for $30,000. The statements gave her no indication to whom they were made out.

The most telling feature of the statement, however, was the positive balance at the top of the first statement and the negative balance at the bottom of the third.

It had taken Kelsey almost a year, organizing their books to find what she looked at right now.

Withdrawals totaling $80,000 and no idea who they had been made out to.

She found matching entries in the general ledger

she had unearthed from a stack of old newspapers. The entries in the ledger were cryptically labeled, "Cash."

She knew what she would find after these entries. Missed bank payments. Escalating interest. Missed payments to other creditors. Another loan at higher interest to pay off what they owed and the beginning of a downward spiral. The down period her father had blamed for their misfortunes had occurred directly after that. But the restaurant could have weathered that if $80,000 hadn't gone missing.

With shaking fingers she folded up the statement, tucked in the checks and put them back in the folder marked with a date four years previous. She phoned her father. Fortunately he was home. She lost no time in getting in her car and driving over.

"I lent the money to Carter. He said it was for both of them. Will and him." Bill Hartley lit his pipe and sat back, puffing furiously when Kelsey had laid out the statements in front of him, asking about the missing checks.

Kelsey stared at her father, part of her mind processing the information, the other denying it. It had taken the better part of an hour, alternately pleading and threatening to find this out.

Now she wasn't sure she wanted to hear it.

"But you never had anything to do with Will?"

"Not directly. No. I gave the money to Carter. He said Will and he needed it for a down payment on a piece of equipment. They were waiting for a line of credit to come through. Then, Carter said, they would pay me back.''

''What piece of equipment?'' she asked, her voice weak with shock. Surprise.

Bill shrugged, avoiding his daughter's gaze. ''I didn't ask. He's my son-in-law....''

''*Was* your son-in-law,'' Kelsey emphasized.

''Anyhow, I trusted him. Trusted that partner of his.'' Smoke was fairly flowing out of Bill's pipe. ''Carter said Will was going to come by to draw up a loan agreement. 'Cept he didn't. I trusted that man. That was a mistake. Will must have thought when Carter was killed he wouldn't have to pay it back.''

In spite of her bewilderment, Kelsey bristled at what he said about Will. She couldn't believe that he was involved in this. ''I'm sure if Will was involved, he would have done something about it,'' she said, her tone defensive.

''That Will guy phoned here once,'' Bill continued. ''After Carter died. Asking about you. I told him you were gone. Didn't tell him where, though. I couldn't believe his nerve. I asked him about the money then. He just played dumb.''

Kelsey felt a jolt at what her father told her. Will had called here. For her. And all the time she thought he had never thought of her. If her father hadn't given Will her unlisted number, there was no other way he could have contacted her.

But that piece of information fought with what else he said.

''What do you mean, played dumb?''

"Told me he didn't know what I was talking about."

"Maybe he didn't?"

"Sure he did. Carter said to leave the checks blank so's he could put Will's name on them."

"So you didn't make the checks out?"

"No. Carter said Will wanted to put in the name of some numbered company. For tax purposes. I never did see the checks."

"And where are they now?"

"I don't know. They were pulled out of the bank statements when I got them. I only ever balanced the books once a year. They could have disappeared anytime." Bill puffed once more on his pipe. "And don't be getting at me about sloppy bookkeeping, okay?"

Kelsey closed her eyes. What good would reprimanding him do now? All the damage was long done. She wondered if Carter hadn't taken the checks out. Because she had a faint inkling of what had happened to the money. Connie, or possibly some other woman. She felt a sudden rise of anger at Carter, bile rising in her throat.

She also knew that she had to talk to Will.

Talk to him about this money to see if he knew anything about it. And to confront him about what he knew about Carter.

"I've got to go, Dad. We'll settle this later." She got up, picked up the offending statements and paused a moment, looking down at her father.

He refused to meet her eyes, his pipe still firmly between his teeth.

He had been foolish, trusting where he shouldn't have trusted. It had cost him dearly. All Kelsey had to lose, if the restaurant went under, was the time spent on trying to save the restaurant and a job.

He stood to lose everything.

Sympathy warred with frustration.

But love for her father won out. She bent over and kissed the top of his head. "I'll call you later," she said softly. Then she left.

As Kelsey drove back to the restaurant, she glanced at her watch. She had a couple of hours of work yet and then she would pick Chris up from her parents' place.

And then?

Go talk to Will? Find out why he would never talk about Carter.

She pulled up to the restaurant and got out of her car. Just as she did, a truck slowed down by the sign, then pulled into the parking lot.

It was Will.

Kelsey stopped short, her heart plunging in her chest. *Not yet. It's too soon. I'm not ready.*

As the truck pulled up beside her, Kelsey pulled her stiff lips into what she hoped was the replica of a smile.

She hardly dared to contemplate why Will was here again. After yesterday she thought he might be too busy to stop by.

Now, he was here again. But now, she knew

something more than she knew yesterday. And this time, she wasn't going to let him pass her off. He was going to tell her what he knew about her former husband. She needed to know how he felt about Carter.

She tugged her shaking fingers through her unruly hair and checked over her clothing. Blue jeans and a button-down shirt today. Uber casual, she thought, tucking her shirt more firmly in her jeans. Well, it would just have to do.

Taking a deep breath, praying that her pounding heart could not be heard by him, she walked over to his truck.

Will hadn't seen her yet. He was fiddling with something on the seat beside him, a soft frown wrinkling his brow.

Kelsey gave herself a moment to savor the sight of him. Then, as if sensing her regard, he turned.

The frown melted, his mouth lifted in a smile that did those silly things to her stomach. Her heart.

He opened the door and jumped out.

"Hi, there," he said, his dark eyes on her as he closed the door behind him. Kelsey was positively weak-kneed by the time he stood in front of her, his hands holding her upper arms.

His eyes looked her over, his smile welcoming. "I've been looking for you."

Kelsey swallowed, her own emotions battling with her doubts. She really knew so little about him.

"What's the matter?" he asked, brushing a tendril of hair away from her eyes.

Kelsey was unused to this easy display from him and it confused her even more.

"I need to talk to you."

Will canted his head to one side, as if studying her. "That's interesting, because that's why I'm here as well."

Kelsey swallowed, wondering what he wanted to tell her.

"What's the matter? You look a little uptight."

"I am, Will," she said, pulling away from him.

His smile faded. To Kelsey it was as if the sun had slipped behind a cloud. *Give me the right words, Lord,* she prayed. She felt as if she hovered on the brink of something important and she was afraid.

She drew away from him suddenly chilled at the return of his habitual reserve.

"Shall we go inside?" he asked.

She shook her head, afraid that if she did, she would lose her nerve. He held her gaze, and for a moment she saw confusion quickly masked.

Kelsey wanted to erase the faint frown on his forehead. To feel again what she had felt yesterday. The connection.

She wanted nothing else but to forget about this. But she knew that for their sake, she had to hear from him what he knew.

"I was going through some bank statements this morning," she said, fiddling with her hair. She took a slow breath, her father's angry words confusing her. "I found three withdrawals made on the restaurant account for large sums of money." She stopped.

Will was silent and she didn't dare look up at him.

We should have done this inside after all, she thought. This is so impersonal. But she had started and couldn't stop now.

Carefully she sucked in another breath, her heart pounding furiously as she tried to find the right way to ask the question that was burning in her mind.

"I just talked to my father about it. He said he gave the money to Carter. For you." She dared a look at him then.

He pulled back, his lips narrowing, his eyes dark as night and as reclusive.

"What am I supposed to know about it?" He sounded angry. Kelsey knew she had said it wrong.

"I want to know what Carter did with the money, Will. I think you know. And I think you know more about Carter than you're willing to tell me."

Chapter Thirteen

Will didn't move. Didn't say anything.

Kelsey would have given anything to know what was going on behind those shuttered brown eyes.

A vehicle drove by, honking a welcome. Kelsey ignored it, her gaze riveted to Will's.

"What do you want me to say?" he asked, stiffly. "Do you think I know something about that money?"

Kelsey nodded. *Please say something, anything.*

"What do *you* know about the money?" he asked, finally.

Kelsey frowned, trying to understand his sudden retreat. "I know that three checks were drawn on the restaurant's account about four years ago. One for $30,000, the other two for $25,000." She wanted to hold his eyes, but he looked so angry. Fear stabbed through her. Carter had been his partner after all. He had always been so reluctant to talk about him.

No, she reprimanded herself. Don't start doubting. Will isn't involved. Can't be.

She looked away, twisting her hair tighter around her finger. "Carter told my father the money was for you. We don't have the canceled checks, so we don't know who they were made out to."

The oppressive silence pressed them apart, broken only by the mocking cry of a raven overhead. Kelsey's fingers trembled as she waited. Will had to know something, anything about this. If he wouldn't tell her, she could only presume that he was protecting Carter. He was always so reticent when Carter's name came up.

She waited a moment longer, then when she couldn't stand the silence any longer, she looked directly at him.

Then she saw his face. Etched on it was the same expressionless mask as when she saw him the first time. The same harsh reserve.

Kelsey's heart trembled and her throat closed. They were back to the beginning.

"Do you think I took the money?"

Kelsey shook her head, slowly. "No, Will. I don't. But I think you know something about it. I think it has something to do with another woman."

Will closed his eyes, as if to push aside the knowledge. "It shouldn't matter, Kelsey. It's over. I don't know if you can get the money back."

"I don't want the money back. I just want to know where it went."

Will turned away from her, leaning his elbows on the hood of his truck. He rubbed his thumb over his chin as if considering what to say next. "Can I ask you a personal question?" he said.

"Of course you can."

Will's glance skittered over hers and then away. "If Carter were alive and you found out he had been unfaithful, would you take him back if he came to you all apologetic with flowers and tears?"

Kelsey wondered where that came from, wondered why he asked. She hesitated, trying to figure out how to answer this obscure question.

"I remember he always sent you flowers." Will lowered his hand, rested it on the hood of his truck. "You said you liked getting them."

"Of course I did. He was my husband. What wife wouldn't like getting flowers?"

"But you would take him back, wouldn't you?" he said evenly. "In spite of all he did. All he would have to do is show up with flowers and all would be forgiven."

"That's not fair, Will," she replied, her pain growing as she tried to understand where he was going. "I can't respond to that because I'll never face that."

"If he came with flowers, all sorry and apologetic, would you forgive him?" he repeated.

Kelsey took a step back at the anger in Will's

voice. "I've forgiven him already, Will. It's been a long, hard struggle, but I have."

Will clenched his jaw, still staring straight ahead, as if he didn't want to look at her.

"What is this about, Will?" Kelsey shook her head trying to understand. This conversation was heading in a direction she couldn't understand.

"I'm not sure." He plunged his hand through his hair. "I'm not sure I can do this right now."

"What do you mean? What's going on?"

"I'm sorry, Kelsey. I've got to go. I need to think."

He strode around to the front of his truck, jumped in and without looking at her reversed out of the parking lot, tires spinning.

Kelsey felt a knot of pain twist in her stomach. What had happened? How could everything have gone so wrong?

Kelsey blew her nose and pushed some papers around on her desk. She felt like a coward and a fool. Too vulnerable, she thought. Too vulnerable by half. She knew that falling in love with Will would put her in that position. And now she was in a limbo of uncertainty.

She pulled a sheaf of papers off her answering machine, dismayed to note the blinking light. She hadn't checked it all day. She was tempted to ignore it, but her quickening heart told her that maybe it might be Will.

Pressing the button, she pulled out a pen and a piece of paper, ready to take down the messages.

The first one was the bank. They had called yesterday to discuss the closing off of the accounts. Bankruptcy proceedings. She hit the button to erase that one.

The next message was from a salesman offering to give them a wonderful deal on restaurant furniture. Was Kelsey Swain interested in a brochure?

"I don't think so," Kelsey said out loud hitting the button again.

The next one was a very excited Maryanne DeGier, the real estate agent Kelsey had contacted. "I found a buyer for the restaurant, Kelsey. Call me right away." The machine gave out the date and time.

First thing this morning.

Kelsey's eyes flew to the clock on the wall as she picked up the phone. With trembling fingers she punched in Maryanne's number, taking a deep breath to calm her erratic heart.

"Hi, Maryanne. I'm returning your call."

"Well, I'm sure this isn't news for you anymore, but the restaurant is officially sold. He signed the agreement for sale late this afternoon. But you probably already know."

Kelsey's heart slowed, thudded once, then sped up. "He? Know what?"

"I thought that's why Will went to the restaurant right after he came here...." Maryanne's voice trailed off.

"What does Will have to do with this?"

"Why, he bought it. The restaurant. Didn't he tell you?"

Kelsey couldn't pull together one single idea. Will? Bought the restaurant?

"Are you there, Kelsey?"

"Yes. Yes, I am."

"I'll give you the number."

Kelsey picked up a pen with shaking fingers. She scribbled the number, still stupefied by what Maryanne had to say.

"And congratulations again," Maryanne added. "He seemed quite excited about the idea when he came in. He's a wonderful man, Kelsey. Not to mention good-looking."

Kelsey nodded dully, then realized that Maryanne couldn't hear that. "Yes. Thanks again. Goodbye." She slowly replaced the phone in the cradle, staring sightlessly at it.

Why did he do that? What did it mean? Why didn't he tell her?

The questions spun around like a flock of snowbirds scared up in the winter—madly off in all directions. She had to talk to him again. Had to dare to confront him one more time. To finish the conversation they had stumbled through just moments ago.

Kelsey picked up the phone, staring at the number she had printed out on a piece of paper. Did she dare call? She held the phone, winged up a quick prayer and dialed Will's number before any more doubts surfaced to confuse and disconcert her.

"Drew here."

"Oh, I'm sorry. I have the wrong number." How in the world had she done that?

"No, you don't. I've got Will's cell phone. Is this Kelsey?"

"Yes, it is." She sounded breathless she realized. Breathless and scared.

"Do you want to leave a message for Will?"

"Yes…actually, no. I should talk to him myself."

"I heard he bought your restaurant. Congratulations."

Kelsey wanted nothing more than to hang up, but considering what Drew had just brought up, it would be rude to simply say goodbye.

"I just heard myself." She hesitated, thinking. If Drew knew about the restaurant, that meant Will had told him. And if Drew knew about the restaurant, maybe he knew a few other things, as well. "Drew, where is Will right now?"

"I dunno. Haven't seen him."

"So, can you tell me…" She paused, biting her lip. She couldn't do this.

"Tell you what?" Drew's voice was quieter. "What is it you want to know?"

Everything.

"Did you ever work with Carter?" Kelsey finally asked.

"Yes. I didn't know him personally. Carter often worked the other jobs with another foreman. I've worked with him, though. Spent time after hours with him a couple of times.''

Kelsey swallowed, pressing her fingers against her eyes. "Drew, don't tell me if you can't, but…" She paused again, wondering if she was doing the right thing. "But I need to know something about Carter. Something about some money he borrowed from my father. He told my father it was for Will. I tried to talk to Will about it, but he won't tell me." The words, once started, rushed out.

"You don't think Will used the money, do you?" Even over the phone Kelsey could hear the condemnation in Drew's tone.

"No. I don't," she said firmly. "I'm pretty sure Carter used it without Will's knowledge." Kelsey felt the all too familiar surge of humiliation saying even this much to a complete stranger. But nothing mattered now. Not her pride, not Carter's treacherous behavior. All that mattered was Will and why he had done what he had. "And I'm pretty sure Carter used it for a woman."

Drew was quiet a moment, his silence confirming what Kelsey had guessed at.

"Was her name Connie?" Kelsey continued, determined to find out.

"Yes. And that's all I'm going to tell you. You don't need to hit yourself over the head with this. Carter was a fool, Kelsey."

"Why wouldn't Will tell me?"

Silence hummed as Kelsey waited, clutching the phone.

"He wouldn't tell you, for the same reason he bought your restaurant."

"And why is that?"

"Because he loves you."

The words were just sounds, disembodied, unattached to a person, words pouring in through an earpiece.

But those four words, those few sounds, changed everything.

She sagged back against the chair, pressing her hand to her mouth. Then, without even saying goodbye, she flung the phone onto the receiver, spun her chair around and flew out of her office.

"I'm looking for Will Dempsey."

The flag girl glanced down at her and nodded. "I'll see if anyone knows where he is." She lifted her boxlike radio to her mouth, and mumbled a few unintelligible words, listened while it squawked back at her.

"Go half a kilometer past here," she said finally. "You'll see some numbers spray painted on the road. Look for number 467. He's parked close to there. Green truck. White markings."

"Thanks." Kelsey pushed the button to roll the window up and once again, it refused to comply. But this time she didn't care. As she drove, she prayed, her heart thumping with a mixture of fear and anticipation.

Drew's words replayed themselves in her mind

over and over again. She clung to them, hoarded them.

She wanted to hear them from Will himself.

Finally she saw a green truck. She pulled up behind it and as she turned off the car, was dismayed to feel her fingers shaking. She made a fist, opened it and then, after winging up another prayer, got out of the car.

The first thing she heard was the assault of the noise of diesel engines worked to the max. She glanced at the cab of Will's truck, but it was empty.

Raindrops spattered here and there on the road. Kelsey glanced up at dark clouds, rolling in fast and low.

Another truck pulled alongside and the driver rolled down the window. "Who you looking for?" he called out.

"Will Dempsey," Kelsey shouted above the noise of the screaming Caterpillars and earthmovers.

"He'll be back in about fifteen, twenty minutes. You want to wait?"

Kelsey's senses were assaulted by the blast of noise. All the troubles and stresses of the past few days mixed in her pounding head. She couldn't talk to Will here.

Then she remembered the cabin and the peace she had felt there.

She turned back to the driver of the truck. "I'll just leave a note for him in his truck. But if you see him, can you ask him to meet Kelsey Swain at the little cabin at the other end of the job?"

"I know which one you mean. I'll tell him." He smiled at her and rolled up his window as he drove away.

Kelsey rubbed her cold arms, shivering in the gathering cool. She stepped hesitantly into Will's truck and closed the door behind her. The cab smelled of a combination of diesel overlaid with the faint scent of his aftershave. She felt a clench in the pit of her stomach at the familiar smell and missed him with a growing yearning.

A clipboard with a pen clipped to it lay on the dashboard and Kelsey picked it up. The first page was filled with Will's notes. Kelsey smiled as she looked them over. She had never seen his handwriting. Precise and definite. Like him, she thought looking at the sharp lines. She turned the page over.

Her heart stopped when she saw the next one.

On it was written "Kelsey." Not once. Not twice, but again and again. He had doodled around each one, swirling lines and straight.

She traced the writing, the swirls, wondering what this meant—a practical man like Will indulging in a moment of frivolity reminiscent of schoolboys.

She smiled, feeling as if she had received an affirmation as she turned the page over. The next one was empty.

On it she wrote, "Please meet me at the cabin you showed to Chris. I know where it is. I'll be waiting."

She signed her name carefully, as if putting all her love into the two words she wrote below it.

Love, Kelsey.

Chapter Fourteen

"**I**'m sure it was this trail," Kelsey muttered, turning down the fork. She had been at the cabin and had waited awhile, but when the rain started, she had decided to go back to her car. The rain had turned the mud around her vehicle to a soup and she couldn't drive it out. The car's window was still down and wouldn't roll up. Waiting in the car would be a wet proposition.

So she decided to go back to the cabin and sit inside.

But the rain had disoriented her. According to her calculations she should have been at the cabin already.

The pelting rain made it difficult to see, to get her bearings. By the time she came to another fork in the road she had to admit that she was hopelessly lost. She had turned back, hoping to retrace her steps.

That was twenty minutes ago and she still hadn't found the cabin.

Kelsey shivered again, and turned around, her hair wet, clinging to her damp cheeks. She had no idea of north or south. No concept of which direction she was traveling.

As she walked back down the path, she searched for worn trails that might lead to the cabin, anything that would give her some indication of where she was. But the rain obscured her vision, changed the look of everything.

"C'mon, Kelsey, you found the place once, surely you can find it again," she muttered shaking her head at her stupidity. Her feet were already soaking wet, and the wet denim of her pants clung to her legs. Rain dripped off her hair and down the back of her coat.

It was growing darker with each step and the rain wasn't letting up. If anything, it was getting worse. Occasionally muffled thunder rumbled overhead.

Please Lord, let me find this place soon, she prayed, hugging herself against the chill. Panic curled around the edges of her mind, waiting. She fought it off, knowing that if she panicked, she would run and if she did that...

Kelsey shivered, as rivulets of water trickled down her back bringing back harsh reality. The longer she walked around the colder she got. If she had matches she could build a fire at least.

I don't have matches.

I don't have anything.

She stopped to look around, hoping something would look familiar, would register. For all she knew, she was walking around in circles.

Her wet feet were now like ice, her hands were numb with cold and she shivered constantly. In northern Alberta even a summer rain brought cold weather. The temperature could still drop considerably at night.

Don't panic, don't panic. Keep moving or you'll get too cold.

But how would Will find her? How would he know where to look if she kept moving? He could keep missing her completely. She slowed, her shivering becoming more intense now as she tried to think.

She broke off a branch from a spruce tree along the trail and laid it with numb hands against the base of the tree.

Then she walked a little farther and did the same with the next one. She didn't know if Will would find her this way, but at least she was marking a trail, giving herself some kind of direction.

"Kelsey. Kelsey, where are you?" Will paused, waiting. But all he could hear was the steady dripping of rain through the trees.

He got her message half an hour ago and that was a good hour after she had been to his truck. Her car was parked in the ditch. Stuck.

He had run to the cabin, his heart in his throat, rain streaming down his face. With each pounding footfall, her words echoed. *Love, Kelsey. Love, Kelsey.*

But she wasn't at the cabin.

The dirt path was already slippery and shiny with rain and all he could see were intermittent tracks.

He had worked back to the fork in the trail and gone down the other way.

He saw a faint mark of a running shoe, and guessed it to be hers. She had taken the wrong trail. Hopefully she had stayed on this one and not wandered down another one.

"Kelsey," he called again, his voice becoming more urgent. The rain was pouring down. Fortunately he had a raincoat and wondered what Kelsey was wearing. He calculated she'd been out in this rain for an hour and a half already.

It was a cold rain. Staying out in it too long would be dangerous.

Please, Lord. Help me find her. Please, Lord. His prayer came easily. Always easy to pray in times of trouble, he thought.

Please, Lord. Help me.

He stopped, and lifted his hands to his mouth. "Kelsey."

Half an hour later, just as he was getting ready to go back to call up a search team, he found a branch broken off and leaning carefully against a tree. A few steps farther, another one.

Kelsey couldn't go on. She could hardly feel her feet or her hands and she had stopped shivering.

She sank to the wet ground, thoroughly drenched and thoroughly scared.

I didn't have a chance to tell Will I love him. I didn't have a chance to say goodbye to Chris. Please, Lord. Please, don't let this happen to him. Don't let him be all alone. Don't let this happen. Not like this.

She huddled into a little ball, desperately trying to preserve what precious little warmth she had as she channeled all her energy into her prayer.

The relentless rain hissed down, dripping down her hair, her neck. She had nothing left in her.

"Kelsey." The faint sound drifted through the rain.

She was getting delusional. She thought she heard someone call her name. She waited.

Then, there it was again. Closer.

"Kelsey!"

She hardly dared to lift her head. Hardly dared to believe that someone had found her.

Then someone dropped to the ground beside her. "Kelsey. Thank the Lord." Warm hands pulled on hers, lifted her face.

And then she looked straight into the welcoming warmth of Will's eyes.

She couldn't say anything as gratitude replaced her fear, her prayers half-coherent.

"C'mon, we've got to get you someplace warm and dry."

She just stared at him, unable to respond.

"You've got to stand up." He pulled her to her feet but she couldn't feel her feet and collapsed.

"Oh, Kelsey. Oh, sweetheart."

Then she felt one arm across her back, his other under her knees. He swept her up against him.

She tried to make her hands respond, but they just hung, useless.

"I've got to get you to that cabin," he muttered. "Talk to me, Kelsey."

The rain still poured down, her feet were still numb, she could barely feel her hands but none of it mattered anymore. She wasn't alone. Will had come for her.

"Kelsey." He gave her a shake. "Say something. Talk to me."

"Thanks for finding me," she said weakly, laying her head against his neck.

"We'll be at the cabin pretty soon. Stay with me."

She couldn't talk anymore, but felt his urgency. Branches slapped at them, spraying even more water. Will stumbled a couple of times on the wet ground.

She was only aware of movement, of the cold hiss of rain and through all that, of being held by Will. He was frowning again, water dripping down his face, plastering his dark hair against his head.

She didn't know how long it took. A couple of times Will set her down to make her walk, to get her circulation going. She could manage for a while, then she would stumble and he would pick her up again.

The whole time he talked to her. She murmured her response, just thankful she wasn't alone anymore.

Then finally he announced, "We're here, Kelsey." He stopped, looking down at her. "I have to set you down so I can open the door. Are you going to be able to stand?"

Her lips were numb so she just nodded.

Carefully he set her down, still supporting her with his arm, as he worked the door open. He strode inside the darkened cabin and laid her on the bed.

She pulled her knees up to her chest, wrapped her arms around them.

She was vaguely aware of him rummaging around, then he knelt beside the bed, stroking her wet hair away from her face.

His eyes were coal-black in the dim light, his narrow brows tightly frowning. "I found some blankets for you. You have to take off your wet clothes and wrap yourself in them. I'm going outside to get some wood for a fire."

Kelsey heard the words as they slowly settled into her mind. She shivered once, then again, unable to stop the tremors that shook her.

"Kelsey, did you hear me?"

She nodded, but that wasn't good enough. Carefully he lifted her up and began to take her coat off. "You have to do the rest Kelsey. I have to get a fire going."

"I will." She looked up at him as another shiver racked her body. "Thanks for finding me."

He just shook his head, then bending over, touched his mouth lightly to her forehead. "I'll be right back. Let me know when you're done."

He opened the door, letting in light and the steady sound of rain dripping. He closed the door with a soft click as light and sound disappeared.

Kelsey fumbled with the buttons of her shirt, her insensate fingers disobeying her mind. She struggled with the wet denim of her pants, barely able to maneuver around the shivering that ravaged her body. Finally she had them heaped in a pile on the floor. She wrapped a blanket around her like a sarong then pulled another around her thoroughly chilled body, feeling, if anything, even colder than before. But inside, a slow warmth was kindling. Will had come looking for her. Will had found her.

She heard a discreet knock at the door.

"It's okay," she said through stiff lips as she huddled in a ball on the bed. "Come in."

The door swung open, letting in a slurry of cold air which was shut off again when Will shut the door. "How are you doing?" he asked as he dumped the kindling and chopped wood on the floor.

"I'm so cold," she mumbled. She felt foolish for complaining. How could she complain? Will was here.

"I'll have a fire going in a flash."

Kelsey closed her eyes, comforted by the sounds he made. The tinny twang as he opened the stove lid, the crumpling of paper, the hollow thunk of wood dropped into the small airtight heater. Then the hiss of a match. The feeling of being taken care of. Someone else was in charge.

She heard the rough scrape of a chair across the floor and she opened her eyes to see him laying her wet pants and shirt across the back of it.

"Here, sit up." Will was beside her now, lifting her up to a sitting position. He picked up another blanket and rubbed the moisture from her hair. She had important things she wanted to tell him, things she needed to say, but all her attention was on trying to control the shivering.

He had finished with her hair and picked up her hands. "My goodness, they're like ice," he muttered.

She watched him bent over her hands, bemused by his attention.

"How did you find me?" she managed to ask past her chattering teeth.

Will looked up at her, his eyes intent. "I prayed and I looked and then I prayed some more."

"I was praying, too," she said, clutching the blanket.

Will closed his eyes and then, finally, he pulled her against him, tight and hard, rocking her. "Oh, Kelsey. I was so worried when I realized that you weren't in your car, and you weren't at the cabin. I saw your footprints all over the place and didn't know which direction to start looking."

His arms around her, his words of concern combined to create a haven that Kelsey didn't think she would ever discover on earth. "I got all turned around," she said.

"I noticed. A couple more minutes and I was going to call the crew down to help look." He pressed a kiss to her wet temple. "I'm so glad I found you," he whispered.

The fire snapped in the stove, its orange glow shining through the open air intake, heat slowly pressing the chill away.

"I am, too." She stopped, surprised at the tears that threatened. Reaction, she suspected.

He drew his head slightly back, his hand cupping her face. She pressed her cheek against its rough warmth.

"Are you getting any warmer?" he asked.

"A bit." Another tremor vibrated through her.

"Here, scoot back, I'll try to get your feet warm."

At first she felt nothing, just the sensation of her feet enveloped in his hands. Then sharp pains shot through them. Her toenails started aching.

She winced.

"Sorry," he said, glancing up at her.

In the late-afternoon gloom his eyes gleamed like two dark chips of obsidian. His disheveled hair and the faint shadow of whiskers on his chin gave him a menacing air.

But she knew better. Will might look like a bandit now, but she knew who he was.

Her hero.

Her hero who had come to her rescue, in so many different ways.

She smiled, pulling the blanket closer around her. The heat of the stove finally reached her. Will rubbed the circulation back into her feet and slowly the shivering subsided.

They had said nothing to each other for the past ten minutes, Will quietly massaging her feet and Kelsey trying to suppress the chattering of her teeth.

She watched him, bent over her feet, his hands working over them. It seemed a menial task, yet he didn't stop.

"You're a very good man, Will Dempsey," she said finally.

Will shrugged the comment off, his eyes lowered. "I don't know if I am, Kelsey."

"Why do you say that?"

Will didn't reply.

Kelsey reached out and caught him by the arm, determined to see this through. Neither of them could leave now. "Why did you leave this afternoon? After we talked about Carter?" It was time, Kelsey thought. Time to get this tangle of half-voiced suspicions and secrets out of the way.

Will stopped, still holding her one foot in his hand as his eyes flicked up to hers. "Why do you need to know?"

"No, Will. You aren't going to answer a question with a question. I think you're hiding something about Carter and I want to know why you are."

He looked down at her foot again, then slowly

caressed it with his thumb. "You love him, don't you?"

"I *loved* him," Kelsey stressed. "He was my husband and I made promises to him." She hesitated. "I didn't always love him the way I should, but I did love him."

"What if you knew the truth about him?"

Kelsey felt again the fear from this afternoon. Fear of saying the wrong thing. But if she and Will were going to go anywhere, if he loved her as Drew told her, if she loved him as she thought, then she had to trust that love enough to be honest with him.

"I know part of the truth," she replied, her voice a quiet sound over the gently snapping fire. "I know about a woman named Connie. I know that Lorelei made some allegations. And I wouldn't doubt they were true." Kelsey stopped, still trying to deal with the hurt from all that. "I'm guessing that the money from the insurance went to one of those women, Connie I suspect. And I'm guessing you knew all of this before you came to Stratton."

Will's fingers lightly caressed her foot as his shoulders lifted in a sigh. "I'm not one hundred percent sure what he did with the money. But I heard rumors of a house he bought in Calgary. I'm figuring it was for Connie. I wanted to tell you what I knew. But whenever you talked about Carter, I knew you still cared about him. I didn't think you knew everything." He released her foot and looked back up at her.

"Only for the past seven months."

Will pulled his lip between his teeth, as if considering his next question. "But you still talked so positively about him."

Kelsey knew her guess was correct. Will thought she still loved Carter. "I had Chris to think about," she said. "For a couple of years, after Carter died, I wanted to make sure Chris knew who his father was. I wanted him to have a sense of where he belonged and who he belonged to. I couldn't suddenly stop that." She took his hand between hers, holding it tightly. "Even though I knew my husband had not been faithful, even though someone could say he didn't deserve to be remembered, I still felt I owed it to Chris to let him have something of his father."

"My mother said she loved my father, too." Will's eyes flickered to Kelsey's then away, as if going back to another place. "My father said he loved my mother. He would lose his temper. Get angry. Then he would beat her for whatever trivial thing had happened. Every time, after that, he would bring her flowers and he would cry and he would beg her to take him back. And she would. She could have bruises and she would still take him back. When I asked her why, she said it was because she loved him." Will stopped and took a deep breath, as if to calm himself. "That's not the kind of love I want."

Kelsey cringed at the anger in his voice. Anger laced with pain.

Please, Lord, help me show him. Give me the right words. She held his hand, touching the calluses on his palm, the marks on the backs of his hand. The hands of a workingman. The hands of an honest man.

"I'm not like your mother, Will. I would never have let any relationship I was in get that far."

Will frowned up at her, shaking his head. "How do you know that? How do you know what kind of relationship you and Carter would have had if you had stayed with him?"

Kelsey shook her head. "I don't. And I've struggled with how I felt about Carter a lot in the past few months," she said quietly, tracing a ridged scar that ran across the back of his hand. "I wondered how I could have been so blind, so stupid. I felt humiliated and cheap. Then when Lorelei confronted me in my own restaurant, I thought I had felt everything. And I forgave him again."

Will's fingers closed over hers, hard. "Can you forgive him now? Can you forgive him for taking money from your father and for putting you through all of this?"

Kelsey bit her lip, feeling once again the anger that had engulfed her when she found out what her father had done with all that money. She took a slow breath, praying as she did so. "It isn't easy. And I deal with it again and again, but I have to."

Will held her gaze a moment longer, then got up from the bed. He opened the stove and threw another piece of wood in, his face lit up by the orange glow of the fire. He checked her clothes and turned them over.

"They'll be dry pretty soon," he commented.

Kelsey pulled the blanket closer around her and leaned back against the wall, the delicious warmth of the fire stealing over her. She watched him fuss around the stove, keeping his distance once again.

Will slowly turned to face her then, his eyes burning in the half light. "Why do you have to forgive him?"

Kelsey chose her words carefully, striving to tell the absolute truth. "Each time I was confronted with what Carter had done I knew I could do two things. I could either let anger take over my life, or I could, with God's help, forgive him and carry on."

"And if he was alive?"

"If he was alive and I knew what I know now, I would first try to save what we had. If he didn't want to do that, I'd have to prayerfully consider my other options."

Will seemed to relax at that. "But you still feel you have to forgive him?"

"Yes. I have to, Will. I've been blind where Carter is concerned. He's dead, and I want him out of the way in every way possible. And forgiving him does that. It takes away any power he might have over me. Over us." She took in a slow breath, feeling defenseless now against her feelings for Will. "I don't want anything, anything at all to stand between us."

In two strides Will was at her side, his hands on her arms. "He was a fool, Kelsey. A blind, selfish fool."

"Yes. He was. But you're not. And you are the one that matters."

"But you still have his picture on your desk?"

Kelsey let a melancholy smile tilt up her mouth. "If you look closer at that picture, you'll see that it's one of you and Carter. I have that picture because it's the only one I have of you."

"What are you trying to tell me, Kelsey?"

"I'm trying to tell you that you are more important to me than Carter ever was," she continued, looking him straight in the eyes. No secrets. No holding back. "I'm trying to say that what I feel for you is stronger than anything I ever felt for him. I know you're not into commitment and permanence, but I guess I'm hoping that when you bought my restaurant, you were trying to tell me something."

She forced herself to look at him, relief filling her at finally being able to tell him. At least partly.

"I could tell you that when I found out about the insurance money I felt an obligation," he said reaching out and taking her hand in his. "An obligation I wanted to deal with that first time I took you out for supper."

"But you didn't say anything then."

Will shrugged, toying with her fingers. "I wanted to, but didn't want to wreck the mood." He looked back up at her. "A woman who won't even let a friend give her five dollars for groceries would hardly accept a few thousand dollars."

Kelsey smiled, squeezing his hand in hers. "You're probably right."

"I could say I bought the restaurant because I'm a businessman, and I think it will prove to be a wise investment. I could tell you it was because I felt sorry for you...." He pressed a kiss to her hand.

"But those aren't the reasons?"

Will smiled one of his rare smiles and Kelsey felt it shiver down into her very soul. "No. They aren't," he said. "I bought it because I wanted to help you and I wanted to show you what you mean to me. It was my own strange way of saying this." He cupped her chin in his hand, his eyes delving into hers, serious, intent. "I love you, Kelsey Swain."

Kelsey closed her eyes to stop the moment, to savor the sound of his words, to try to see them in her mind.

"I love you." He laughed shortly as he said it again. "I've loved you for a long, long time."

She felt his fingers caress her chin, felt his lips touch her face as she let his words fill an emptiness that only he could fill. Finally she opened her eyes, losing herself in the dark, soft depths of his. "I love you, too, Will," she whispered, pressing her hand against his. "I think I have for a while."

Then, finally, he lowered his mouth to hers, their lips touching, sealing their love.

He drew her close then, tucking her head under his head, his chest lifting in a sigh.

He said nothing as he rubbed his chin over her damp hair, back and forth, his arms a hard, warm sanctuary.

"My own Kelsey," he said finally, his words a rumble under her cheek. "I've cared for you longer than I dare admit."

"How long?" she asked.

"I think since the first time I saw you." He stroked her head with his chin again, his hand rubbing circles on her back.

She lay still as she went back to that day, surprise making her momentarily speechless.

"Then already," she said finally.

"Yes. Disreputable person that I was."

"I remember you from then."

"No, you don't. You only had eyes for Carter."

"Your hair was longer than now," she continued as if she hadn't heard him, toying with the top button of his shirt. "You needed a shave," she said, her voice growing soft as she remembered. "You wore a lined plaid flannel shirt. It was red, and you wore it over another shirt. A work shirt with snaps. Your work boots weren't laced up. They were leather. Tan leather with a rip in one toe. I could see the metal from the steel toe. But what I remember most was the frown. You always wore a frown."

Will became perfectly still.

"I paid way too much attention to you, but you were so distant," Kelsey continued finally able to speak of the things she had held back so long.

"You scared me."

Kelsey pulled back, surprised. "How could I do that?"

Will pressed a quick kiss on her hair. "I remember you stopping by my table and touching me. I remember how light your touch was, like you really cared if I was enjoying my meal. You do that so easily,'' Will said, his tone sorrowful. ''Just a light touch and you've made that connection. Such a small thing, touching…hugging…''

Kelsey heard pain in his voice and instinctively reached out to him, letting her fingers drift down his face. Touching him. ''Did your parents never hug you?''

Will's eyes flicked over her face, his expression suddenly serious. He shook his head. ''Maybe when I was a baby. I can't remember.''

''You said that your father used to strike your mother. Did he ever hit you?''

Will's mouth twisted into a bitter smile. ''Not when I was older.''

''What about your mother?''

''My poor mother was too busy just trying to survive the marriage, let alone pay a whole lot of attention to me.'' He stopped. ''I survived it, Kelsey. I don't want any pity from you.''

Kelsey leaned forward and brushed her lips against his. ''I only want to give you love,'' she said, her voice breaking with sorrow for the emptiness that Will had experienced in his life. She gave him another kiss. And another. ''And I have lots to give you.''

Will's eyes drifted shut as he took what she gave.

Then he took her face in his hands, his eyes traveling over her features. ''I've discovered so much since you've come back into my life. Love, faith, emotions..." He smiled. "I've realized that a life without God, without love is so empty." He stroked her cheek with his thumb. "I wish I knew how to show you...how to tell you what you mean to me."

"You already have, Will," she said quietly. "You already have."

Chapter Fifteen

❦

"You can come in now," Kelsey called out, pulling Will's coat over her still-damp shirt. Her clothes weren't completely dry, but she had to get back home. Back to Chris. Back to her parents.

Back to reality.

Kelsey looked around the cabin, still trying to absorb what had transpired here. Secrets had been brushed away, hearts had been opened. She wanted to hold on to this moment. Forever.

Thank you, Lord, for this blessing, she prayed as she snapped up Will's coat. *Thank you for this time out of time. Help us through whatever lies ahead.* She felt a moment of indecisive fear and prayed it away. God would help her and Will through this. As long as they continued to trust in Him.

The door opened and Will stepped inside, bringing in an armful of firewood. "It's still raining out there," he said with a shiver as he knelt down. He stacked up the blocks, ready for the next time the stove would need lighting.

He stood close to the stove, rubbing his hands. "Soak up the heat while you can because you're going to get chilled again on the trip out."

"How far is it to the truck?"

"About a twenty-minute walk." Will gently tucked a strand of hair behind her ear. "Are you sure you're up to it?"

Kelsey smiled, warmed by his solicitousness. How long had it been since she'd had a man fuss over her? She brushed aside the memory of Carter. In spite of all his overt care, she had never felt protected by him. Safe with him. Not the way she felt with Will right now.

"As long as you're with me, I think I'll be okay," she said catching his hand and pressing it to her cheek.

Will hugged her hard. "I'll be beside you every step of the way. 'Though she stumble she will not fall, for the Lord upholds her with His hand.'" he quoted.

Kelsey frowned. "And that's from…?"

"One of the Psalms, I think. I read it just the other night. Except I paraphrased it. I memorized it because I know I've stumbled lots in my life." His expression became serious. "I'm really thankful that God brought you into my life, Kelsey. He knew I needed you."

His intense gaze held a hunger that she only began to understand.

With her fingers, she gently feathered away the frown that pulled his eyebrows together, then traced their straight lines.

"And I need you, Will Dempsey," she said softly, trailing her fingertips down his cheek.

His features softened and he lowered his head, touching his lips gently to hers. "I love you," he whispered.

"And I love you," she said. "I don't know if I can stop saying it."

"Sounds good to me." Will gave her another quick hug, then took her hand in his. "We should go."

The walk back to the truck was brisk. A few times Kelsey wasn't sure which way they were going, but she clung to Will's hand and let him lead her. His steps were sure and didn't falter.

The rain had eased off some, but nonetheless she was shivering again by the time the trees thinned out and they reached the road.

Her car was sitting in the mud, its window still open, the driver's seat glistening with moisture.

"You forgot to close the window," Will said, stating the obvious as he reached in and tested the driver's seat.

"It won't shut. It's stuck open."

"You can't drive that back even if we manage to pull it out," Will said as took her purse from the passenger seat. "You'll get chilled with that open window. Give me the keys and I'll make sure it gets back to you.''

Kelsey pulled the keys out of her pocket and handed them to Will in exchange for her purse. It was wet as well and probably ruined, she thought as she opened it up. Thankfully her wallet was still dry.

"Let's get to the truck, Kelsey." Will caught her hand and helped her through the sticky clay mud to his truck.

"Think you'll get out of here?" she asked, looking with dismay at all the mud around them.

"I'm not worried," he said, helping her into the truck.

Then she didn't need to be, either, she thought watching him as he walked around the front, one hand on the hood.

He got in, flashed her a quick smile and put the truck in gear. Tires spun and the engine roared as they rolled backward. Then forward, then backward, mud spinning up and hitting the windshield, the side windows and spraying all around. All the while Will worked the gearshift, his other hand on the steering wheel, his movements quick and sure. Then, with a final scream of the engine, it climbed up the incline to the road.

Safe.

She cleared aside the papers and the miscellaneous items that separated them, and set herself beside Will, tucking her arm in his.

"Are you okay?"

"I'm fine, Will."

But in spite of that, he reached over and turned the heat up.

"Do you want to phone your parents and tell them you'll be a little late?"

"I'm not too far off the mark," she said glancing at the dashboard clock. It was six o'clock. "If the restaurant is really busy, I often don't pick up Chris until six-thirty. No sense getting them all worried."

Silence enveloped them, broken only by the hum of the tires on the wet pavement, the occasional remnant of dirt being flung up behind them.

Kelsey laid her head on Will's shoulder, feeling distinctly proprietary. "So now you own my dad's restaurant, what are you going to do with it?"

"I thought I'd get this amazingly beautiful, warmhearted, intelligent redhead to manage it for me," Will said. "And who knows? Maybe with a few renovations and a few changes, business could really pick up."

Kelsey smiled. "And where do you expect to find this paragon of virtue?"

Will tilted her a quick glance. "I already found her. And when she gets home and picks up her son, I thought I could take the two of them out for supper and we could discuss the future."

"As in...?" Kelsey asked teasingly.

"When we should start on renovations, for one thing."

Kelsey smiled though it was a little forced. It wasn't quite what she had in mind, but she was willing to take things slow with Will. "Of course.

That's important." She stroked his arm, reminding herself of his declaration just moments ago.

"I think so, too." Will smiled down at her and then turned his eyes back to the road as they headed toward Stratton and Chris.

Kelsey turned off the computer and sighed lightly. She didn't know why she had foolishly thought that once Will bought the restaurant, all her problems would be solved. Instead she had spent the past three weeks talking with an architect, making decisions on interior design and trying to figure out which direction she wanted the restaurant to go.

And that was the easy part, she thought, scowling at the blank computer screen. Will had brought her office up to speed by computerizing it. Thankfully she had taken computer courses in college and could still remember the basics of the accounting program that Will had bought.

She rubbed her forehead, willing away the headache that prowled around the edges.

She wasn't supposed to get them anymore. Will's love, Will's financial rescue was supposed to be the answer, the happy-ever-after to her life.

Will had swept into the restaurant, making things happen, getting things started. The bank wasn't on her back anymore, but she dealt each day with more decisions than she had to make before Will's financial rescue.

Forgive me, Lord, for being so ungrateful, she

prayed, pressing her cool hands to her heated cheeks. *Forgive me for wanting more than I have.*

It was hard not to. Will had been gone for the past week and a half and she missed him terribly. He phoned every other night and they shared information. He told her about the job in Drayton Valley that was almost done, and she told him what new things were happening in the restaurant.

It seemed cold, sterile and Kelsey didn't know how to change it. How to reach out to him over something as detached as a phone call. She yearned to see him face-to-face, to touch him. To hear his deep voice tell her once again that he loved her. Not to discuss how their respective jobs were faring.

She couldn't say she wasn't warned, she thought. She knew Will wasn't one for idle chitchat. Will's love ran deeper than that, she reminded herself. She smiled remembering his rescue that day in the rain. Her hero.

But the memory brought again the ache of missing him. She had to get going, that was all. Will was supposed to come home in a couple of days. Then they could talk face-to-face. In his last phone call he said he had something he needed to discuss with her.

Sighing lightly, she got up from her chair and slipped her cardigan over her short-sleeved sweater. She gave the office a quick glance, making sure everything was ready for Monday. She closed the door behind her, looked around the restaurant and frowned.

The restaurant was full, which wasn't unusual for this time on a Friday night, but what caught her attention was the unusual quiet. A number of people were looking in her direction, smiling.

Puzzled, she returned the smiles, looking around to see what the joke was. But as far as she could see, the joke seemed to be her.

"Okay," she said smiling gamely back. "What is going on."

"Come on over here and find out," Anton called out slapping his hand on his knee.

"Don't be shy," Cory yelled from another corner of the restaurant.

Confusion warred with humor, but then, with another laugh, Kelsey walked toward Anton.

From the booth across from his table, someone stood up.

Kelsey's heart did a little dance and her steps quickened as she recognized the dark head. He turned toward her.

"Will? What are you doing here?" She ran toward him, flung her arms around him.

He picked her up, held her close, murmured her name. Then, oblivious to the staring patrons, the whistles and catcalls from others, he kissed her.

Finally he lowered her to the floor, his dark eyes hungrily staring at her. "I missed you, Kelsey. So much," he whispered in a voice heavy with yearning.

"I missed you, too," she said, bracketing his face

with her hands. She couldn't look at him enough.
Couldn't hold him hard enough.

But he drew away, taking her hands from his face.
He kissed them once, then dropped them.

He glanced around at the people in the restaurant
who were now avidly staring at the two of them.

Then he looked back at her.

"What's going on, Will?" she asked.

Will looked over his shoulder again, signaling.

She could hear light laughter and then Chris ap-
peared, walking toward her, carrying a long cardboard tube.

He grinned at the people watching him, then back
at his mother. Stopping in front of his mother, he
took another quick look around, enjoying this small
moment of fame.

"Here, Mom. This is from Will. For you. I got to
give it to you." Chris grinned from ear to ear as he
handed her the long cardboard tube.

Kelsey gave Will a puzzled frown.

"Open it," he urged.

She brought it to the table and pulled the plastic
end off the tube. A faint flower scent mixed with
cardboard floated out.

She tipped the tube sideways and a single red rose
slipped out onto the table. Bemused, she picked it
up, then noticed a white silk ribbon tied to the stem.

Her heart stopped and she felt her throat thicken
with tears as she saw the diamond solitaire ring tied
to the ribbon.

She glanced at Will, hardly daring to understand.

Will took the flower, took her hand and got down on one knee in front of her.

"Kelsey, my dear love. You know this is not my style, but I'm doing this because I know it is yours." He grinned at her, his thumb stroking her knuckles. "Will you marry me?"

She could hardly see him through the tears that pooled in her eyes. Could hardly hear the shouts of the restaurant patrons through the roaring in her ears.

She let one quick sob escape, dashed the tears from her cheeks and nodded, unable to speak past the happiness that filled her heart.

"Yes, I will," she whispered, squeezing his hands so tightly, it hurt.

Will got up and gently drew her toward him again. "Don't cry, Kelsey," he said softly. "It's okay."

He handed the rose to Chris who was filled with self-importance. "Can you take that ring off that ribbon and give it to your mom?" Will asked.

Chris looked appropriately solemn and laying the flower on the table, carefully untied the ribbon. "Here, Mom," he said handing her the ring.

But Will took it and with a smile that lit up his whole face, gently slipped it on her finger.

"There's more, there's more," Chris crowed, jumping up and down in excitement.

Kelsey palmed the tears away from her cheeks, unable to stop the smile that made her face ache.

"What more could I possibly want?" she asked, clinging to Will's hand.

"Go ahead, Chris," Will said gesturing to the cardboard tube with his free hand.

Chris reached in and pulled out a roll of paper, as long as the tube was and laid it on the table.

Will drew Kelsey closer to the table, as other people began to gather behind them to see this new development.

"What is this?" Kelsey asked, now thoroughly puzzled, bamboozled and just plain overwhelmed.

Will drew his hand out of hers and unrolled the paper. He set a sugar container on one corner and a napkin container on the other to keep the paper from curling back.

"What do you think?" he asked, slipping an arm around her shoulder.

Chris was standing on the bench. "It's just a bunch of funny lines," he said, puzzled.

Kelsey leaned over the paper and finally understood. "They're house plans," she said carefully.

"For our new house," Will said.

Kelsey stared down at the blueprint, her finger tracing the lines of the living room, bedrooms, kitchen. There were two stories.

"I'm tired of living in my trailer," Will said, squeezing her shoulder.

Kelsey didn't think she could possibly absorb anything more.

"See, and this big room here. This is going to be

my office." Will glanced sidelong at her, his expression puzzled at her lack of response. "I decided to make Stratton my home base. I don't want to be on the road anymore."

Kelsey wanted to assure him, but couldn't say anything, couldn't control the emotions that overwhelmed her.

Finally she couldn't hold them back any longer.

She dropped into the chair behind her, covered her face with her hand and burst into tears.

The only sound in the suddenly quiet restaurant was the sound of her muffled sobs.

"Kelsey, honey. What's wrong?" Cory was beside her in a flash, her hand stroking Kelsey's arm.

Kelsey looked up at Cory, managed a tremulous smile at Chris then beheld the confused puzzlement of Will's face.

"I don't think I can get any happier," she sobbed.

Will glanced at Cory, as if looking for reassurance.

"This is a good thing, Will," Cory assured him, pulling Kelsey to her feet.

Kelsey threw her arms around Will, still sobbing, totally unashamed of her display of emotion.

"I love you, I love you, I love you," she cried, not caring who heard, not caring who saw.

Will held her tight, rocking her lightly. "I love you, too, Kelsey," he whispered in her ear. "Everything about you." Then as he kissed her again, the restaurant burst into shouts of congratulation.

* * *

Later, at Kelsey's home, they laid the blueprint out on the floor of the living room, going over every room, every part of the plan.

Chris asked questions galore and Will patiently answered them.

"If there's anything you want to change, Kels, just say so." Will glanced up at Kelsey who knelt beside the paper, her eyes glowing.

"No. I love it just the way it is."

Will grinned back at her. "I know I took a chance going ahead and getting them drawn up, but I wanted to come with something concrete. I wanted to wait until the other job was done and until I could do this all together. I wanted to do it right."

Kelsey grinned back at him and leaning over, dropped a light kiss on his forehead. "You did wonderful, Will. Such a romantic." She smiled into his soft-brown eyes, then glanced back at the prosaic blueprint that represented so much more. "Will it work out for you? To not be on-site?" she asked.

"Of course. I'll have to head out to the jobs at times, but I don't intend on staying longer than necessary. I'm going to be scaling down. Keeping only one crew going. I think we'll be able to live off that plus what the restaurant makes." He had done all his homework on this. Had done the projections for both the business and the restaurant. And he had prayed.

Kelsey sighed, stroking his face with her hand. "I

don't deserve you, Will Dempsey. Rescuer of damsels in distress and all-around hero.''

"Don't say that, Kelsey.'' He caught her hand, pressing a quick kiss to it. "You gave me more than I can ever hope to give you.''

Chris looked up, his face screwed up in puzzlement. "Are you guys going to do that all the time?''

"Do what?'' Kelsey asked.

"All that kissing stuff,'' he said with a disgusted tone.

"Come here, sport.'' Kelsey dragged him toward her.

He didn't protest and climbed onto her lap. Kelsey then grabbed Will's arm and pulled him beside her.

"We are going to be a family,'' Kelsey said, leaning her head against Will. "And we're going to be a family that hugs and kisses and tickles.'' She dug her fingers into Chris's side and he bent double laughing.

She looked at Will, her expression serious.

Will felt his heart expand with love, thankfulness and praise as he sent up a prayer of thanks.

"We're going to be a family,'' Will agreed, wrapping his arms around his future wife. His future son. "We're going to be a family that loves God, and loves each other. And shows it.''

And he did.

* * * * *

Dear Reader,

Kelsey and Will needed each other, though they didn't think so at first. Kelsey needed Will's stability and Will needed Kelsey's giving nature. They had to learn this by getting to know each other, by taking the time to see life through the other's eyes.

We don't need to be the same. We don't need to respond to God exactly the same. But when we are open to how God speaks to each of us individually, I think we can learn from each other.

Carolyne Aarsen

P.S. I love to hear from my readers. Write me at Box 114, Neerlandia, Alberta T0G 1R0.